KILL IN PLAIN SIGHT
BY
REMINGTON KANE

KILL IN PLAIN SIGHT
Copyright © REMINGTON KANE, 2015
YEAR ZERO PUBLISHING
978-1-937120-77-1

LEARN ABOUT NEW RELEASES FROM
REMINGTON KANE

http://www.remingtonkane.com/contact.html

CHAPTER 1- Tanner to the rescue

Tanner jammed the tip of his blade into the base of the first man's skull, causing the second man to swear in surprise. After ripping the blade free, Tanner pivoted and sliced open the second man's throat.

That move kept the man from shouting, while also causing him to abandon all thoughts about the gun he was reaching for, as his hands flew to his throat in a feeble attempt to stem the rich gush of blood.

Tanner then stepped over the body of the first thug, even as the second thug slid down along the side of the car he and the other man had arrived in, an old Cadillac with New York plates.

Once past the men, Tanner stood in the open and waved both arms in a beckoning gesture towards the camera, which was set high above a door marked, RECEIVING.

He was in the town of Washington, New Jersey, and it was just after midnight on a Sunday.

Tanner was in the town's warehouse district, which consisted of over a dozen new monolithic buildings that were roughly the size of football fields.

The building he stood before housed an electrical supply chain's main warehouse, and there was a man hiding inside named Tim Jackson.

Jackson was a computer hacker with a price on his head, however, Tanner wasn't there to kill him, but to save him, and to do that, he would have to kill the hit squad that was after Jackson, a hit squad sent by The Conglomerate.

Tanner lowered his arms and quit waving. Either Jackson had seen him take out the two men and clear a path for escape or he hadn't. If he wasn't watching, there were three more men to deal with, one each for the three remaining sides of the building.

The two men he had just killed had been tasked with keeping an eye on the rear of the huge building, which had over sixty bay doors, two exit doors, and a wide metal door that went up on rollers. Had the hacker, Tim Jackson, exited by any of those doors, he would have been cut down and killed.

The other three sides of the building had only one door each to exit by. The door on the left side of the building led to a side parking lot, and a short stretch of grass dividing the property from its neighbor, which was another massive warehouse.

The door on the right led to a field of grass that was bordered by a fifteen-foot high sound wall, beyond which was the New Jersey Turnpike, and in the front of the building were glass doors leading to a lobby, and the office area beyond.

Cameras gave a view of all sides and Tanner assumed that Jackson had seen the hit squad approach and surround him, and was either glued to the monitors or hiding in the warehouse.

Hiding wouldn't have done Tim Jackson any good, the five men would have entered the building, blocked all exits, and hunted him down.

But now the men had become the hunted, and it was Tanner who hunted them.

Tanner stripped off the black hoodie he'd been wearing, the second man, the man with the gashed throat, had spewed blood all over it, and anyway, Tanner needed to change.

The first man wore a New York Yankees cap along with a matching jacket, and Tanner stripped them off the dead man and put them on, pulling the cap low. The man had also been wielding a sawed-off shotgun, and Tanner picked it up, checked the load, and carried it with the barrel pointed towards the ground, as he headed to the right side of the building.

Tanner walked with his head lowered slightly, to obscure his face, and hoped that the jacket and cap would cause the man stationed on the right side of the building to assume he was the man he'd taken them from.

It worked, and Tanner made it within twenty feet of the man before he heard him speak in a hushed tone.

"Shit, you ain't Mikey."

"Mikey's dead," Tanner whispered, as he dropped the shotgun and brought out the silenced pistol.

The first shot caught the man just in front of the left ear, while the second entered his open mouth and exited in a spray of blood.

The body made even less sound than the silenced shots as it tumbled to the grass, and Tanner scooped up the shotgun and headed towards the front, where he hoped to deceive yet again.

It was not to be.

The man guarding the front doors was sharp, and likely the crew leader. He was a man in his forties with a graying goatee, and he pegged Tanner as a phony within moments of spotting him.

Tanner was watching the man from under the bill of the cap, and when he saw the man's gun arm come up, he fired off a blast from the shotgun.

The steel pellets went wide of the man, but did make him dive behind an air-conditioning unit. Tanner pumped the shotgun and sent a second blast towards the front doors, to shatter the glass, before making his way inside the dark building.

As he went behind the reception desk, he heard the man outside calling for his troops, and then the bitter curses that followed when he discovered that only one of his men remained.

Tanner pushed through the door behind the reception area, moved past rows of desks, and listened at a window that faced the parking lot.

When he heard a new voice speaking in a whisper, he chanced a look out between the slats of the window blind, and could see the lower leg of one man jutting out from beyond the air-conditioning unit, as both men hid behind it on their knees.

Tanner took out the silenced gun, pressed its muzzle against the glass, and took aim.

When he pulled the trigger, the scream told him that he had hit the man, and although the wound would be far from fatal, it would still slow the man down and cause him to bleed, and those that bled were often more fearful than dangerous.

The men returned fire, shattering what was left of the window, but Tanner was already rushing back towards the entrance, pumping the shotgun as he ran.

He emerged from the building with the shotgun held up and found the crew leader helping his wounded man along, as they moved around the air-conditioning unit and away from the window.

Tanner and the crew leader fired at the same moment, and Tanner felt a tug at the left sleeve of the Yankees' jacket, while the blast from the shotgun just barely reached its targets and blew holes in their feet and ankles.

Both men tumbled to the ground, grunting in pain, and Tanner pumped and fired again from a dead run, the blast hitting one man in the throat, killing him, while a stray pellet stung the left shoulder of the crew leader.

The crew leader fired and the bullet passed through the spot where Tanner had been, but Tanner had dived to the ground, while releasing the shotgun, and rolled to the crew leader's left.

The crew leader had to shove the last of his men out of the way to make a shot, and that gave Tanner all the time he needed to free his gun, take aim, and fire.

The crew leader let out a scream, dropped his gun, and used both hands to check out the devastation inflicted on his face. Tanner's shot had entered the man's left cheek and made a neat hole, but had exited the right cheek in a spray of blood, teeth, and tongue.

The crew leader rose to his knees, his eyes filled with pain and horror, as his fingers turned crimson, and he mumbled guttural sounds that were meant to be words.

When Tanner stood over him, he saw the terror in the man's eyes turn to hate.

Tanner nodded, placed his gun against the man's forehead, and ended things.

Afterward, he stood listening for several minutes.

It was an early Sunday morning and the warehouse district was as quiet as a graveyard. If not for the subdued hum of the traffic drifting over the sound wall from the turnpike, the night would have been filled with only the sound of crickets.

The hacker, Tim Jackson, had disabled the building's alarm system, and Tanner supposed that there was no one close enough to have heard the sound of gunfire.

After hearing not a hint of a siren, nor seeing the flash of police lights in the distance, Tanner walked back towards the entrance to go in search of Tim Jackson.

He had just saved the man from certain death, and if he was right, Jackson could return the favor. The hacker was the key to Tanner surviving the war with The Conglomerate, for this was the information age, and the right info was worth more than a thousand guns.

Tanner shed the pinstriped Yankee apparel, crunched broken glass beneath his feet as he reentered the building, and found Tim Jackson twenty minutes later, as the man cowered beneath a desk in the shipping manager's office.

The young man gazed up at Tanner with wide brown eyes as he shivered with fear.

"Please... don't kill me."

Tanner offered his hand.

"We have to talk."

CHAPTER 2 - Batmen & Robin

Summervale, North Carolina, outside the main gate of the Reynolds Lumber Mill

Jerome Green poured the last of the coffee from his thermos and swallowed the lukewarm liquid in two gulps. Gripped in the crook of one arm was the sign he was carrying, the sign read, REYNOLDS IS UNFAIR!

Jerome was black, athletic, thirty-seven, and the married father of three children. He had worked at Reynolds Lumber since college, when he put in full-time hours during the summer.

Carter Reynolds, the former octogenarian owner of the mill, had been one of Jerome's best friends, despite the difference in their ages, but after Carter's death two years ago, everything changed at *Reynolds*.

Carter's widow, Arleen, had promoted Jerome from Office Manager to General Manager, but Arleen died of a stroke just a month after her husband's death, and the mill passed on to a grandson who sold it to an out of state corporation.

Jerome and everyone else at the mill were given a steep reduction in pay. Those that complained were told to leave, while those who stayed were worked harder.

That was when Jerome called his older brother, Rafe. Rafe Green was a former army MP who became a union organizer, and with his brother's help, Jerome was determined to unionize *Reynolds* and make it a good place to work again.

The New York City corporation that owned the mill fought against unionization, but a large majority of the workers voted for it during an official and State-monitored election, and Jerome asked for a meeting with management to discuss contract talks. The new owners demoted Jerome instead, and that caused the rest of the workers to walk out and form a picket line.

The strike had been going on for three weeks, and in that time, there had been two minor skirmishes between the strikers and the security professionals hired to protect the property.

Tonight there would be a third skirmish, but it won't be minor, and will be instigated by a different breed of professional, the professional thug.

Jerome was watching the gate with two other men, to keep out replacement workers. Although he was their unofficial leader, he volunteered to work an overnight shift like everyone else.

He was thinking about the trip to the zoo he planned to take with his kids later, when the five men in ski masks came out of the woods swinging baseball bats.

Jerome used his sign to knock one of the men off his feet, but was hit from behind by another man. The blow caught him just above the left elbow and he felt his entire arm go numb.

After that, came the blows to the head, followed by pain, followed by blackness.

***

Inside the building, a college freshman named Robin Murphy was gawking at the security monitors, while wincing in sympathy at the beat down he was watching.

KILL IN PLAIN SIGHT By REMINGTON KANE

He was a handsome boy with dark hair and green eyes, tall, but with a thin frame.

"Oh Jesus, they're going to kill those guys."

For all its brutality, the violence didn't last very long, and when the three union workers lay broken and unconscious, Robin roused himself from shock and reached for the phone to call for the police and an ambulance.

Before he could even touch it, it rang.

"Hello?"

"Robin, this is Mr. Trent from New York, do you remember me?"

"Yeah," Robin said. He remembered Al Trent. Al Trent had arrived in a limo and was wearing a suit worth more than Robin's entire wardrobe, so yeah, he remembered him. He also remembered wondering how a man only a year or two older than himself had made so much money and become so important.

"You've had trouble there tonight, yes?"

"Yeah, five guys just beat the crap out of the men who were picketing."

"I see, and have you called anyone yet?"

"No."

"Don't call, it's being handled, but what I do need you to do, is to open the gates wide. We have new workers coming in."

"Scabs?"

"Strikebreakers, men who appreciate the chance to work,"

"Oh, all right, but you're sure an ambulance is coming, because man oh man but those guys took a beating."

"Did you see who beat them?"

"Not really, they were dressed in black and wore masks."

"Well then, it could have been anybody, and to answer your question, yes, an ambulance is on the way, in fact, three of them, but nevermind that, just go open the gates, and Robin?"

"Yes sir?"

"Turn off the camera at the gate for an hour or so, if anyone asks, it malfunctioned."

A long moment of silence passed, and then Robin asked a question.

"Are you telling me to erase what happened, the beating?"

"Not at all, the police need to see that footage, but I am telling you to turn it off now."

"For about an hour?"

"Exactly,"

Robin reached over, hit a switch, and the gate camera cut off.

"I just shut off the camera, Mr. Trent."

"Good man, and remember one more thing, I never called tonight."

"Okay, but you're sure the ambulances are coming?"

"I guarantee it, now go open the gates."

The ambulances had arrived by the time Robin got the gates open. They scooped up Jerome Green and his companions, U-turned in the gravel lot, and rode off just as two large trucks appeared. The trucks were following a Black Hummer, and stopped at the gate when the Hummer's driver paused to speak to Robin.

The driver had a New York accent and he sent Robin a grin. Robin had seen the man before but didn't yet realize it, because at the time, the man had been wearing a ski mask and wielding a bat.

"You talked to Al Trent, kid?"

"Yeah, and he said new workers were coming, is that you guys?"

The man and his four companions laughed, and one of them slapped the driver on the shoulder.

"Hear that Joe, you could have a new career."

The driver smiled and talked to Robin again.

"Nah kid, the new workers are in the trucks. Once they're inside, lock those gates."

Robin nodded that he understood and the small caravan entered.

When the men in the trucks got out, Robin noticed two things about them. They were all Chinese and they all looked scared and desperate.

The driver of the Hummer walked over and gripped Robin's shoulder. He was about forty, with average looks, but Robin could tell by the man's grip that he was strong, and when he spoke, his eyes never left Robin's eyes or even blinked.

"When the cops come, tell them what you saw and give them a copy of the security tape. We'll be in that building towards the back with the new workers, don't mention us to the cops or anyone else, got it?"

Robin nodded, and then followed it with, "Yeah,"

"Good, and here's a little something for you."

The man stuffed money into Robin's shirt pocket and walked away.

When Robin saw that he had been given a thousand dollars, his eyes grew wide and he stared after the man with a sick feeling in his stomach, while wondering what the hell he had been dragged into.

CHAPTER 3 - How much did he eat?

Tanner took Tim Jackson to a 24-hour truck stop in Bordentown, New Jersey, and the two of them talked over cheeseburgers.

Jackson was 23, white, of short stature, and genius IQ. He had been a hacker since the age of eleven and had used his skill for both fun and profit.

That all ended when he inadvertently accessed one of The Conglomerate's offshore accounts.

That was nearly a year ago, and in that time, The Conglomerate had searched for him, trying to figure out who it was that reached through the Internet and dared to rob them. To that end, they employed their own hackers, and three weeks ago, Tim Jackson, AKA Rom Warrior, became known to The Conglomerate.

Skilled at disarming run-of-the-mill alarm systems, Jackson evaded the first man sent to kill him by breaking into a building and using on-site security cameras to stay out of reach and escape. That proved useless tonight with the five-man team, who could cover all exits, and if not for Tanner's interference, Jackson knew he'd be a dead man.

"I want to thank you again for saving me, Tanner, but I am curious about why you did it. You say you want me to steal info for you, what kind of information?"

Tanner looked at Jackson with admiration. The kid had come within minutes of dying and still ate enough for a man twice his size. He had three cheeseburgers, onion rings, French fries, a chocolate shake, and two pieces of rhubarb pie. That appetite was a good sign, he would need nerve to do what Tanner wanted him to do.

"I want you to go undercover," Tanner said.

"Undercover? Where?"

"At MegaZenith, in New York City,"

Jackson squinted at him.

"You're not a cop, so are you a spy?"

"I'm what you would call a hit man."

Jackson laughed, raised his milkshake to his mouth, and then stopped moving, as he studied Tanner's face.

"Shit, you're serious, aren't you?"

"I am."

Tim Jackson put down his milkshake and leaned back in his seat, to ponder over Tanner's revelation.

Tanner gave him time to think things over and gazed around the truck stop. It looked like a slow night, as less than a dozen customers were present, and most of them were seated at the counter, where a flirtatious waitress with large breasts held court. She seemed to be addressing most of the men by name, and Tanner guessed that they were regulars, such as truckers that drove the same long distance routes week-to-week.

Tim let out a sigh, and Tanner brought his gaze back to him.

"If you were going to kill me you would have done it by now, so what is your game?"

"The Conglomerate wants me dead too, but I plan to make that too expensive for them. If you can get into MegaZenith and get what we need to blackmail them, they'll be forced to leave us alone."

"What is it you're after?"

"Their books, they likely call it something else, but they must keep records of their financial transactions, their *real* financial transactions, and once we have that, we'll have them."

Jackson had been slurping his milkshake through a straw as he listened, but Tanner's words caused him to cough and sputter.

After wiping his mouth with a napkin, he spoke to Tanner in a measured tone.

"I don't know how computer savvy you are, but what you want is impossible. If those records exist, you can be certain that they're protected by high-level encryption, and that's something that even I couldn't break."

"You could if you had enough time though, couldn't you?"

"Maybe, but it could take years to break such encryption, and even then it would be sheer luck."

"Luck would have nothing to do with it, by going undercover at MegaZenith you might gain access to information that can help you break their encryption."

"Let's say you're right, but that also means I'll be going inside a place where the order to have me killed came from, what if I'm recognized?"

"You'll be hiding in plain sight, they'll never connect you to your false identity."

"Still, they want me bad enough to send five guys after me, they won't stop until I'm dead."

"That's true, but you'll also be put on the back burner soon."

"How do you know that?"

Tanner smiled without warmth.

"I'm about to become their top priority."

CHAPTER 4 - The Sharpe sisters

In the SoHo district of Manhattan, Sara Blake entered the storefront office of an independent newspaper called *Street View*.

The weekly paper began as a blog written by two college students who were sisters, Emily and Amy Sharpe.

The Sharpe sisters had a taste of fame and success years earlier when they were the first to report on a blockbuster story.

A friend of theirs mentioned that she thought her boss was crooked. The boss in question was a well-respected man with an honorable history who seemed beyond reproach. This man managed a hedge fund worth over twenty Billion dollars.

The Sharpe sisters went back to writing their daily blog that dealt with Wall Street and which specialized in giving a financial world-view from a twenty-something perspective.

Their friend returned to them in tears one day with the news that she had been fired. Apparently, her boss had heard that she was spreading unfounded rumors and sullying his reputation.

When the friend opened her purse and produced several documents she had copied from her employer's files, the Sharpe sisters realized that their friend was telling the truth.

They went with the story on their blog, and lit a firestorm in financial circles, and by the end of the day, they were neck deep in threats of lawsuits and defamation charges by the fund manager's attorneys.

The sisters then posted the documents their friend had supplied them with and all hell broke loose on Wall Street. The SEC, the FBI, and every major news outlet became involved, and within a week, the fund manager was vilified and in cuffs, while the Sharpe sisters became celebrated and admired.

That was eight years ago.

Since that time, *Street View* had become just another financial blog limping along, but it had also enabled the Sharpe sisters to eke out a living in one of the most expensive cities in the world.

***

Emily Sharpe looked over at her sister, Amy, and then back at Sara Blake.

"Would you say that again please?"

"I said I'd like to buy *Street View*, and that I'm willing to keep you on as managing editors and contributors."

"But we're not selling," Amy said. Like her older sister, Amy was a dark-haired beauty with blue eyes and a thin, but shapely, figure. Both women were unmarried, although Emily was divorced after a brief marriage that occurred during college.

Sara smiled at the sisters.

"I have information that will blow the financial world away, but it's an emerging story, and I may need your help in developing it fully."

"Are you a journalist?" Emily asked.

"No, I'm a former FBI agent, however, I did minor in journalism in college."

"Just how much were you willing to pay?" Amy asked.

Sara mentioned a figure as well as the salary the sisters would receive, and Emily and Amy exchanged another look as their eyes widened. They then asked Sara to excuse them as they retreated to a corner of the small office to talk.

The offices of *Street View* had once been a boutique that specialized in handbags. It was a narrow space a dozen yards deep, with a bathroom and closet in the rear, beside a door that led to an alley where deliveries were off-loaded.

There were two desks towards the back that faced each other, while in the front was a reception area with several chairs, a coffee table, and a sofa. It was this area where Sara was meeting with the Sharpes.

The sisters returned and sat across from Sara.

"That's a very generous offer," Emily said, "But I'm afraid we'll have to pass."

"May I ask why?"

"We don't want to be employees ever again," Emily said.

"I see, but you would still be running things."

"We like being in control, and we did found this paper, well, we founded a blog, but it became a weekly newspaper as well," Amy said.

"I think I could make *Street View* a force again," Sara said, then added, "No offense,"

"No offense taken," Emily said. "The glory days of *Street View* are obviously behind us."

They grew quiet as Sara considered their words.

"I have a second offer. Let me buy in at forty-nine percent, while you each keep twenty-five and a half, that way, you'll maintain controlling interest and I don't have to pay your salary."

"That's a better offer," Emily admitted. "But we couldn't get by on half of what we make."

"I understand, and I won't take any proceeds until the business generates a net profit that's double what you currently make."

"Are you serious?" the sisters said in stereo.

"Yes I am."

The Sharpe sisters excused themselves again, and when they returned, Emily extended her hand to Sara.

"We accept, send us a formal offer under those terms and we'll pass it on to our lawyer to look at."

"All right, but I want to move fast on this, very fast."

"This story you say you have, can you give us a hint?"

"I'll just say this, the underworld and the financial world have been getting cozy."

"You have proof of this?"

"No hard evidence as yet, but I uncovered this in my former role as an FBI agent."

"This is dynamite, isn't it?" Amy asked.

"Yes, and it will attract attention, does that frighten you?"

The sisters grinned.

"Hell Sara, we live for it."

CHAPTER 5 - The Brothers Dim

Brooklyn, New York

Hours later, Sara watched as Merle and Earl Carter wandered among the cars in the parking lot of a supermarket.

It was the third parking lot she had followed them to, and while she at first thought that they were searching for a particular model of car to steal, she soon realized that they were looking for an easy car to steal, one where the owner had left the vehicle unlocked and the keys inside.

That told her that they had no skill as car thieves, but it also told her that they were persistent. She had been filming them from her own car, and when Earl signaled to his older brother, she knew that they had at last gotten lucky.

She started her engine and moved towards their position slowly, while keeping the camera trained on them. After Merle joined his brother and they backed their stolen prize out of its

KILL IN PLAIN SIGHT By REMINGTON KANE

parking spot, she put the camcorder down and blocked their exit by driving directly at them.

Earl avoided a head-on collision by slamming on the brakes, and the two brothers glared at her through the windshield of their stolen car.

When Merle recognized her, he turned to his brother and said three words.

"She's a Fed."

Sara pointed back at the parking space the boys had just pulled out of, and with a sigh, Earl backed the vehicle into it. Whether or not, the car's absent-minded owner would have returned and realized the vehicle was facing the other way was anyone's guess, but the brothers left the car with the keys in it, and trudged over towards Sara.

She had parked her car as well, and when they reached her, she showed them the video of their felony.

Merle looked up from the camcorder screen and gazed around in confusion.

"Where's all the other Feds?"

Sara smiled at him.

"Luckily for you I'm no longer in law-enforcement, but I can hand over this video to them at any time."

Earl had been staring at her legs, but he raised his eyes and asked a question.

"What do you want from us, lady?"

"Tanner, I want to find Tanner, and you two are going to help me do just that."

Merle and Earl raised their hands and waved them as if they were refusing seconds at a cookout.

"No way," Merle said. "That damn Tanner almost got us killed, and it's a miracle he didn't do it himself. Hand in that damn video and we'll take our chances."

"I'm willing to pay," Sara said, and saw a spark of interest enter the brothers' eyes.

"How much?" Merle said.

"One thousand a month, and all I want you to do is to keep your eyes and ears open and let me know if you hear any news on Tanner."

"A grand a month for that, that's it?"

"Yes, but you'll also need to put yourselves where you'll be likely to hear such news."

Earl squinted at her.

"And where would that be?"

"You need to get in close with Johnny R, he wants Tanner dead for what he did to his uncle, Rossetti, and he's the best chance I have to track Tanner down."

Merle shook his head.

"Johnny R is a made man, he'd never hang with me and Earl."

"I don't need you to become his best friends, but I do need you to become part of his organization, that way, you'll be in a position to hear things."

Merle pointed back at the car they had stolen.

"We were going to take that to one of Johnny R's chop shops, once we get there, we could bullshit and maybe learn something."

Sara stared at the three-year-old Volvo the boys had stolen. After coming to a decision, she took out a slip of paper that had a cell phone number written on it. She held out the paper and spoke to Merle.

"Take the damn car and give me a call at that number when you hear anything."

Merle took the slip of paper and grinned.

"What about the money?"

"Come up with some info and I'll give you your first payment."

Merle and Earl exchanged glances and something unsaid passed between them.

"We want more than a grand, how about six-hundred for each of us?"

Sara smiled her agreement. When she said a thousand a month, she had been talking about a thousand apiece, the brothers had just bargained themselves into getting less money.

"I want to hear from you soon, you got it?"

"Yes ma'am, we don't like Tanner either, but what are you gonna do once you find him?"

Sara stared at them with cold eyes.

"I'm going to make that bastard wish he had never been born."

The brothers exchanged glances again, and this time the thought they shared was one of gratitude. They were grateful that they weren't Tanner, for they had no doubt that Sara meant to make her words come true.

CHAPTER 6 - Go to New York and die

Rafe Green felt his mother tremble as she sobbed against his chest, as they stood beside his brother's bed.

Jerome Green lay in a coma after the beating he received at the Reynolds Lumber Mill, and the doctors didn't know if he would ever awaken.

Rafe caught his sister's eye and she nodded in understanding, and afterwards, she guided their mother away to the cafeteria where she could pull herself together.

That left him alone with his sister-in-law, and he hoped to get answers from her.

"What have the cops said about this, Rita?"

Rita Green gazed up at him with red-rimmed eyes.

"Jerome and the other men were beaten by five men dressed in black and wearing ski masks, they even have video, but they can't identify them."

"The last time I spoke to Jerome he told me that *Reynolds* had hired a new security firm, and he also mentioned that a man named Monroe had tried to intimidate them."

Rita nodded. She was a light-skinned black woman with large hazel eyes and long hair.

"I asked the Sheriff about that, and he said that those security people all have alibis. They were seen drinking in the *Tree Top Pub* until closing, even that man, Monroe, and so it must have been someone else that did this to Jerome."

"*Reynolds* hired outsiders to cover for their outsiders, it's clever, and I would guess they assume that no one will ever be able to prove anything."

Rita sniffled.

"I don't care who hurt him. I just want Jerome to get better."

Rafe bent over and kissed the top of his sister-in-law's head.

"Jerome's tough, baby, you'll see, he'll come out of this coma, and in the meantime don't worry about a thing. If you need money or help with the kids, the family is here for you."

Rita took his hand and gave it a squeeze.

"Thank you, Rafe."

Rafe left Rita with Jerome and headed for his car. He needed answers and was going to get them one way or another,

***

Chuck Monroe lived in an apartment complex in Summervale that catered to young professionals. At forty-one, Monroe was pushing the young part, and as hired muscle, he was also not what most would consider a professional, but Monroe liked the building, and had dated more than one of his young female neighbors.

Monroe had a bodybuilder's physique, wore jeans and T-shirts, and kept his blond crewcut ultra short, so that the gray at his temples was less noticeable.

Around his apartment building, he was known as a man you didn't mess with, but the morning after Jerome Green was beaten into a coma, Monroe's reputation took a serious beating as well.

Monroe walked towards his car in the parking lot of his complex and found Rafe sitting on the hood.

"Hey buddy, get off my damn car."

"My name is Rafe Green. I'm Jerome Green's brother."

"Yo, Green, I didn't lay a finger on your brother, ask anyone, I was at the pub until closing."

"So I heard, but you know something about what happened, and I'm not leaving here until you tell me what that is."

Monroe stepped closer to Rafe and glared with malice.

"Get the fuck off my car before you get hurt."

Rafe had been leaning back on the car, a blue, vintage Pontiac Firebird, with his palms flat on the hood. His weight shifted onto his left hand, as his right fist caught Monroe on the chin. Monroe took a step back, shook his head, and threw a right of his own.

Rafe was off the car and blocked the punch, and then delivered a second punch to Monroe's midsection, followed by a third, fourth, and fifth, in rapid succession.

Monroe dropped to his knees and barfed up the bagel and eggs he had eaten for breakfast.

Two of his neighbors stood by staring at him, both were young women nearly half his age, and when Monroe saw the laughter in their eyes, it hurt more than Rafe's punches had, because he knew that the story of his beating would spread and make him the butt of jokes.

In a fit of rage, he jumped to his feet and lunged at Rafe. Rafe stepped aside with ease and Monroe landed atop the hood of the Trans Am.

Rafe bent down and whispered into his ear.

"You're a big, strong guy, but you have little skill. I'm trained in both Karate and Judo, and as an Army MP, I handled guys like you as a matter of course. Stop fighting, tell me what you know, and keep at least some of your dignity."

Rafe straightened and waited. Monroe lay atop the hood for a few seconds, before turning over and sliding down into a position much like the one Rafe was in when Monroe first saw him.

"New York City,"

"What about New York City?"

"The guys that hurt your brother were from New York. I don't know their names, but I heard that the crew leader was named Joe Puller, or something like that."

"Anything else?"

"Yeah, they're mob guys."

"Mob? Like the Mafia?"

Monroe shrugged his massive shoulders.

"That's what I heard, so brother or not, you might want to drop it."

"They hurt my brother, there's no dropping it, and if you're thinking of telling anybody about this conversation, I wouldn't. They might consider you a loose end, and they also don't like snitches."

Monroe gave him a look of hatred.

"Go to New York, you'll die there,"

"We'll see," Rafe said, and then he walked past the pair of gawking young ladies, climbed in his car, and headed home to prepare for his trip to New York.

CHAPTER 7 - Semper Fi

Days later, with preparations made and his family coming to terms with dealing with his brother's condition, Rafe loaded his suitcases into his car.

He was going to New York City to deal with the people who had hurt his brother, and was just about to leave, when John Murphy parked across the street and exited his jeep, with Murphy was his son, Robin.

Rafe knew both of them because John and Robin Murphy were members of the same church his mother attended, and Rafe and John had worked together on a charity drive. They also shared a military background. Rafe was Army, while John had been a Marine.

Rafe shook both their hands while noticing that Robin looked uneasy.

"What's up, guys?"

John gestured at Rafe's apartment. He looked like an older, more world- weary version of his son, and his dark hair had streaks of gray.

"Why don't we go in and talk."

With beer and soft drinks in hand, John encouraged Robin to begin, and the boy told Rafe everything he knew about the night his brother was beaten.

"A Hummer?" Rafe asked Robin.

Robin handed Rafe a New York State license plate number written on a strip of paper.

"It was a black Hummer and that's the plate number, and all five of those guys had New York accents. I saw them again as I was leaving, and I heard them call the young one Carmine, but the one who did most of the talking, he was called Joe."

"And the man who called you, his name was Al Trent?"

"Yes sir,"

"Why didn't you tell this to the cops?"

"I told him not to," John said. "His bosses told him to keep quiet about it as well, and the last thing I want is for Robin to get beaten like Jerome did."

"But you're telling me, why?"

John looked over at his son.

"Robin, please wait for me in the jeep. I'll be right there."

"Okay, Dad, and Mr. Green, I'm sorry about what happened to your brother,"

Robin was nearly at the door when he remembered something. He walked back to Rafe and handed him the money that Joe Pullo had given him.

"They tried to buy me with that. You use it, maybe it will help with your brother's medical cost, at least a little."

Rafe stood and hugged the kid.

"Thanks Robin, for everything,"

After Robin left the apartment, John asked Rafe a question.

"You're going after them, aren't you?"

"I am, and thanks to you and your son I'll have a lot easier time tracking them down."

"They don't strike me as men that would be easy to get the better of, maybe you should rethink things."

Rafe took a deep breath and slowly released it.

"No. I'm going to make the bastards pay, and if possible, I'll prove *Reynolds* was behind the attack."

John sighed.

"Old man Reynolds would be spinning in his grave if he knew what became of his company."

Rafe stood.

"I need to get going. I want to be in New York tonight."

"I wish you luck, brother, and Rafe, don't get yourself killed."

"That's not part of the plan, but nobody fucks with my family and just walks away."

John grinned and punched him on the shoulder.

"Are you sure you weren't a Marine?"

CHAPTER 8 - Daddy's girl

In New York City, Frank Richards left his limo and saw his daughter rushing towards him, her face lit with rage.

One of his bodyguards grabbed her by the arm and stopped her progress, but Richards waved the man off, and Madison Richards kept coming until she was standing before her father. She was Richards' only child from his second wife and had been unwanted by Richards.

The petite young woman had her mother's dark curls, but wore his mother's angelic face, and it was that face that kept Richards from hating her outright. Richards had loved his late mother dearly, and his daughter always reminded him of her, unfortunately, she also reminded him of his late wife, a woman he grew to despise and ordered killed.

"Another one quit, Daddy, did you pay him off too?"

"I don't know what you're talking about."

"The private detective I hired, the third one, as a matter of fact, and he just up and quit for no reason like the other two, only he looked scared, so I guess maybe you threatened him instead of buying him, hmm?"

"You need to stop this insane quest of yours and accept facts. Your mother died in a drunk driving accident. She drank too much and ran off the road."

"Mom wasn't a drunk and there was no reason for her to be out on that back road in the early morning. Why can't you see that there's something odd there?"

Richards took his daughter by the elbow and yanked her to the rear of the limo.

"Enough, Madison! That's enough. Either you accept what happened or I'll toss you to the curb."

"You're disowning me?"

"You've graduated college, gotten your own apartment, you're an adult, but you're not independent. I'll have your car taken away and cancel your accounts. Your mother died in an accident and that's all you need to know."

Madison wiped at tears.

"I know you didn't like each other anymore, that you were getting divorced, but did… did, did you kill her, Daddy? Is that why you're so afraid of learning the truth?"

Richards made a sharp intake of breath and broke eye contact, and Madison backed away from him, as her face crumbled.

"Oh, Daddy, no, no you didn't."

Richards spoke to her, but he still wouldn't meet her gaze.

"Leave, Madison, and don't ever mention your mother again. If you can't do that… then you're no longer my daughter."

Madison sat on the curb and cried, and Richards walked away with his bodyguards flanking him.

***

When Richards entered the MegaZenith Building on Broad Street, Al Trent was waiting for him in the lobby. Trent was twenty-one, but had graduated Harvard at nineteen.

Trent was the son of one of Richards' friends and he had taken him under his wing and found a kindred soul. Al Trent was as cold and merciless as Frank Richards, and had become a confidant and advisor.

They exchanged greetings and then remained silent until they were alone together in Richards' office on the top floor of the sixty-story building.

Richards settled in behind his desk, fired up his computer, and bade Trent to sit across from him.

"Fill me in on what's been happening."

Trent pushed his glasses up farther on his nose and began his report.

"Tim Jackson is still out there somewhere."

"And have we learned who was helping him?"

"Not yet."

"He certainly didn't dispose of those men himself."

"No, he must have hired a group of mercenaries."

Richards looked up from his keyboard.

"Find him again, that little piss ant should have been dealt with easily, and make sure we take care of whoever is helping him as well. What's next?"

"The Summervale problem has been solved. We've replaced the strikers with Chinese laborers."

"Yes, but what about the strikers?"

"Their leader, a man named Jerome Green, is still in a coma. That seems to have taken the fight out of them and ended the picketing. Also, the local police have no way to tie the company to the attack."

"Excellent, anything else?"

"Just the usual—Tanner. We still have no idea where the man is, but he can't hide forever, and when he sticks his neck up, we'll chop it off."

"Contact Johnny R and tell him I want to see progress on that. Tanner disobeyed a direct order from me. That can't be allowed."

"I'll tell him, but you know he wants Tanner dead as much as you do. The man killed his uncle."

"Find Tanner, Trent, find the man and have him dealt with."

Trent nodded his understanding and headed for the door, unaware that Tanner would soon make himself not only easy to find, but impossible to forget.

CHAPTER 9 - That would be best

The following morning, Tanner entered Johnny R's Cabaret Strip Club in Manhattan and saw the bartender's mouth drop open in shock.

It was early, and so the place was closed for business, but the bartender was restocking the shelves with bottles, as an old man swept the floor.

Tanner knew the bartender slightly. His name was Carl, and as Tanner took a seat on a stool, Carl whispered to him.

"Tanner, get the hell out of here, man, Johnny R has a contract out on you."

"How much?"

"Fifty G's is what I hear," Carl said. He was a middle-aged man with Sandy-colored hair and a pleasant face, although his eyes always looked sad.

Tanner tossed his head towards a hallway.

"Is Johnny in?"

"This early? Not hardly, but that kid Richie Sullivan is here, still here actually, he's been with one of the girls in Johnny's office since closing time."

"Sully's kid, what's he like?"

"He's an even bigger prick than Sully was, God rest his soul, but you didn't hear that from me."

"What's he do, run this place with Johnny?"

"The kid has his own crew. They do a few heists, rough up the late payers for Johnny R, stuff like that."

Tanner stared at the bartender.

"I know there's a sawed-off shotgun kept under the bar, don't get any ideas about collecting that contract on me."

Carl backed up with his hands held high.

"Shit, Tanner, that never crossed my mind. Listen, if I had those kind of balls I wouldn't be a bartender."

"But as soon as I walk away you'll call someone, won't you?"

"I... if I didn't they'd kill me."

"Make the call while I go see the kid."

"Are you going to kill Richie?"

"That's up to him."

"I guess, but hey, don't hurt the girl, she's just trying to get by, ya know?"

"I'll send her out."

"Good, you got class Tanner, and balls too, to come in here like this, huge balls."

"Just stay away from that shotgun," Tanner said, and Carl swallowed hard.

He left the bartender, strode down the hallway, and kicked in the door to the office.

There was a large wooden desk across from the door, but on the right was a green leather sofa, and atop the sofa was a naked redhead and a kid that had punk written all over him.

The woman didn't scream, but her eyes were wide with fright, and when she saw the gun in Tanner's hand, she licked at lips that had gone dry.

"Out!" Tanner said, and the woman grabbed a silk robe from the floor and scurried past him and down the hallway.

On the sofa, Richie Sullivan yawned and brushed back his jet-black hair with one hand, while the other reached for his cigarettes. He was wearing a pair of red boxer briefs and nothing else, and his skinny chest was pale, but hairy.

"Who the fuck are you?"

"Tanner."

Richie paused with the cigarette halfway to his lips, but after blinking fast several times, he placed it in his mouth and lit it with a match.

"You're worth a lot a money, Tanner, Johnny R has a hard-on for you. Did you really kill that fat fuck uncle of his?"

"I want you to pass on a message to Johnny R and The Conglomerate."

"I'll bite, what's the message?"

"I'm coming for them. I'll kill Johnny R and Frank Richards, and if anyone gets in my way, I'll kill them too."

Richie laughed around his cigarette.

"I heard you were a badass, but nobody told me you were crazy."

"Just give them the message."

There was a door behind the desk. It opened onto an alleyway that led to the street. Tanner headed for the door, and just as he unlatched the lock, Richie bent down and grabbed a gun that was lying beneath the sofa. As he was bringing it up to fire, Tanner shot him. The bullet hit Richie's hand, all but severing the thumb, and Richie wailed as the gun tumbled back to the floor.

Tanner left him without a backwards glance and walked down the alley, and past stacks of empty liquor bottles. The alley faced a wooden fence, but had a chain link fence on either end, and

Tanner opened the gate set in the middle of it and went out onto the street.

***

Three doors down and across the street was a coffee shop, and Tanner walked inside and joined Tim Jackson at a table near the front.

When Tanner left Jackson, the boy genius was on his second stack of pancakes, and upon his return, Tanner found him eating an omelet. Tim Jackson weighed 150 lbs. at most, and Tanner wondered where the kid put all the food.

The waiter brought Tanner a cup of coffee, and as he took his first sip, a black Cadillac came to a skidding stop in front of the strip club. Five young men emerged, two of which carried shotguns, and all five of them rushed into the club.

Tim Jackson wiped sweat from his forehead.

"Are you sure it's safe to sit here?"

"It is for now. They're used to people running and hiding from them, they'd never think that I would sit and watch them from across the street."

"Why are we watching them?"

"I'm gathering info. I now know what Richie Sullivan's crew looks like. I also know that they're stupid enough to run in a pack instead of spreading out. If I had stayed at the bar, I could have cut them all down as they entered the club."

"This guy, Richie, did you kill him?"

"I shot him in the hand when he pulled a gun. He'll live… for now."

Tim Jackson squirmed in his seat.

"How many people have you killed?"

"I don't count."

"When you take a contract, will you kill anyone? I mean, if a guy wanted his wife dead so he could collect her life insurance, would you do it?"

"I don't take domestic contracts. The people I kill are all guilty of something, even if that something is just bad judgment."

"Does it ever bother you, the killing?"

Tanner placed his cup down atop the table and stared into Tim's eyes.

"We're not that different, it's just that I have a lower threshold than you do."

Tim swallowed once, as Tanner's gazed unnerved him.

"Lower threshold?"

"You would kill to protect someone you love, or to save your own life. With me, the threshold is lower. I'll kill for money."

Tim broke eye contact and Tanner went back to watching the club.

"But it's not just money though, is it?" Tim said. "You don't kill for money any more than I hack into accounts and steal for money. It's more about what the money buys, the freedom, the time to live and not just slave away at some job. And it's also about being who you are. I'm a hacker because I'm good at it and I love doing it, love figuring my way around security measures and firewalls, and you're a killer for the same reasons I'd guess."

Tanner said nothing but gave a slight nod.

Tim gave the subject more thought and asked a question.

"I justify what I do because I only steal from large institutions, and I guess your justification is that you only kill the guilty, am I right?"

"Somewhat, but everyone dies sooner or later, whether they cross my path or not. It's inevitable."

Outside the window, an ambulance arrived, and Richie Sullivan came out of the club surrounded by his crew. They were all young guys who had the cynical and cocky look that all young thugs seem to wear.

Tim wiped more sweat off his brow.

"There are six guys there, you can really kill them all?"

"I will, and then they'll send more, and they'll die too."

"But they'll get tougher and tougher?"

"Yeah, and while I'm keeping them busy, you'll get what we need."

"What if I can't break their encryption?"

"Eventually, they'll find you and kill you."

"And you?"

Tanner drained his coffee cup, and when he sat it down, he locked eyes with Tim again.

"If I have to, I'll just keep killing them, Johnny R, Frank Richards, and whoever comes after that. I'll just keep killing them until I reach the man at the top."

"Or until they kill you?"

"Or that, yes."

"I'll break that encryption, Tanner, somehow,"

"That would be best," Tanner said, and signaled the waiter for more coffee.

CHAPTER 10 - I'm not normal?

Al Trent answered the phone on Frank Richards' desk, said, "Send him up," and placed the receiver back in its cradle.

"Johnny R is here."

"Meet him at the freight elevator and escort him here, but only him, if he has any of his toughs with him, make sure they wait by the elevator."

"Yes sir, and would you like me to sit in on the meeting?"

"Of course, and from now on, you'll be the only one interacting with him. I shouldn't be taking this meeting at all, but I want to make it very clear that Tanner must be handled quickly."

Trent went off to greet Johnny R and found him standing with a fat man wearing a bad suit, who Trent knew was his driver.

Trent hated Johnny R for the simple reason that Madison Richards had once looked at a photo of the thug on the cover of a weekly news magazine, and mentioned that she thought he was "hot". She had never said such a thing about the nerdy Trent, and so Trent hated Johnny since that day. He also loved Madison Richards, who he had known since childhood, but Madison did not return his feelings.

Johnny R had recognized Trent's animosity towards him, but normally ignored it. To Johnny, Trent was just a corporate lackey and nothing more, someone beneath his notice.

Johnny Rossetti, Johnny R, stood a head taller than his late uncle, Al Rossetti, and Johnny was also slim, while his uncle had been rotund. A handsome man who tended to dress well, Johnny R had become a favorite subject of news photographers, and although he would never admit it, he liked seeing his picture in the paper.

He'd been arrested more than once but had only done time as a juvenile offender, and at thirty-eight, he was in a position of power where he never had to dirty his hands.

Johnny R was the new Underboss of the Giacconi Crime Family, a position that placed him only one rung below its leader, Sam Giacconi. But Giacconi was elderly and thought to be senile, leaving Johnny R as the family's perceived leader.

However, that was the old hierarchy, in the new hierarchy of The Conglomerate, Johnny R was mid-level at best.

In The Conglomerate, prissy college boys such as Al Trent were considered his equal, while Blue Bloods like Frank Richards thought themselves his superior.

Frank Richards, who had placed a contract on Johnny's Uncle Al and started the whole Tanner mess in the first place. That hit had been sanctioned, and later rescinded, but Johnny R had a long memory, and someday he would pay Richards back, someday, but for now, he'd play the game.

Trent pointed at the driver.

"He'll have to wait here."

Johnny turned to his man.

"Stay here, Mario, this shouldn't take long."

"You got it, Boss."

As they walked to Richards' office, Johnny voiced his displeasure at being treated second class.

"I don't like this freight elevator shit. Richards doesn't think I'm good enough for the front door?"

"He doesn't want anyone snapping a picture of you entering the building like a normal person."

"What? I'm not normal?"

"No, you're a petty street thug, and Mr. Richards can't be associated with you in public."

Johnny smiled.

"Petty street thug? Are you trying to hurt my feelings, kid?"

"I just call them as I see them."

They reached the office and went in past an empty receptionist desk. The woman who sat there was given an unexpected break from her duties and sent down to the building's commissary.

Johnny R shook Richards' offered hand and sat to the right of Al Trent, as the two of them settled into leather wing chairs in front of Richards' desk.

After brushing a hand across a wrinkle of his blue Armani suit, Johnny R started things off.

"I guess you heard Tanner's message or we wouldn't be meeting."

Richards curled his upper lip in a gesture of disgust.

"Tanner is insane, delusional, or both. I don't know what he hoped to gain by coming out of hiding and issuing that ridiculous declaration of war, but now that he's back in New York, I expect him to be handled within the week."

"My man, Joe Pullo, he tells me that it's no joke. He says if Tanner said he's coming for us, then that's exactly what he means to do."

"This Pullo, does he know Tanner well?"

"Not well, no one knows Tanner well, but he's known him longer than anyone."

Al Trent spoke up and asked a question.

"What's Tanner's first name?"

"Even Pullo doesn't know that. He says Tanner has always gone by that name alone, and he also says that the man has never had a woman that he cared about, or at least no one he'd risk himself over."

"How reliable is this man, Pullo?" Richards asked Johnny R, but was answered by Trent.

"He and his men handled that labor dispute in North Carolina last week, sir, along with a number of other things."

Richards nodded.

"Ah, that man, yes, he seems more than competent. Will he be going after Tanner?"

"Yeah, him and everyone else," Johnny said. "Tanner will be hunted down and killed like the dog he is. The word has been put out to every hooker, junkie, dealer, and bookie there is that Tanner is worth money to whoever fingers him. If he rents a room, buys a drink, or takes a cab, we'll hear about it, and God help the bastard if they take him alive, because then I'll get to him, and I'll make him pay for what he did to my uncle."

"I spoke to Tanner in Las Vegas and tried to talk sense into the man, but he insisted on killing your uncle, perhaps it had become personal to him, but I did try to stop it."

Johnny R lowered his head and stared at Richards with his coal black eyes.

"*After* you ordered it,"

Richards cleared his throat.

"Yes, I ordered it, your uncle had been... uncooperative, but we settled things without violence, and Tanner should have stepped aside."

Johnny R stood.

"Anything else?"

"No, but I meant what I said. I want Tanner dead within the week. His type of insubordination might give others ideas."

"He'll be dead soon, count on it."

Al Trent escorted Johnny R back to the freight elevator, and when he returned, he leaned in the office doorway.

"I don't think Johnny has forgiven you for ordering his uncle's death, despite the fact that you attempted to stop Tanner."

"I realize that," Richards said.

"If his animosity persists, maybe we should do something about that."

"Perhaps," Richards said, "But with any luck, Tanner will kill him before dying himself."

"That would be the best of both worlds," Trent said.

Richards grinned.

"Wouldn't it though?"

CHAPTER 11 - They should have stayed for the concert

That evening found Merle and Earl parked atop stools inside Johnny R's Midtown strip club, and hoping to learn something they could take back to Sara.

When Joe Pullo walked in and took a table towards the back, Merle dragged his gaze away from the topless dancers and told the bartender to send Pullo a drink and ask if they could speak with him.

Once the drink was delivered, Pullo looked over at them with a quizzical expression, but then waved them over to the table.

Merle sat beside his brother and offered his hand. Joe Pullo left it unshaken and asked a question.

"What do you two want?"

"We want to find Tanner, you know, for the reward," Merle said.

"You think you can kill Tanner?"

"We ain't killers, but we got lucky once back in Vegas and grabbed him after he killed a crew that was hunting him down."

Pullo raised an eyebrow as he studied Merle and Earl. His eyebrows were bushy, but at forty-one, his hairline had receded a bit, and if you didn't know what he did for a living, you might guess that he was a college professor, or maybe a doctor, because his eyes held the sharp gleam of high intelligence.

"You two grabbed Tanner out in Vegas and you're still breathing, how did that happen?"

"We got lucky, but we were also at Rossetti's house when Tanner hit him, and that time we got blown up."

Pullo smiled.

"So let me get this straight, you survived Tanner twice, and you're coming back for more? What, you two got a death wish?"

Earl shrugged.

"He's worth fifty G's."

"You boys got more guts than I'd have guessed, but why come to me? I don't know where Tanner is."

Merle leaned closer and spoke in a low voice.

"You run the best crew in the city. As soon as he knows where Tanner is, Johnny R will send you out to kill him. Why not let me and Earl tag along? Like I said before, we ain't killers, but maybe we can sorta herd him your way, and if we help, then we'll share the reward, whatever you think is fair."

Pullo stared at them as he thought things over.

"Give me your phone number and tell me where I can find you. Once I know where Tanner is, maybe I'll call."

Merle gave Pullo the information and stood up, Earl followed suit, and after they said goodbye, they drifted out of the bar.

They talked about Pullo as they walked along in the gathering dusk, and decided to walk through Central Park. With night approaching, people were leaving the park, but there were just as many entering, because there was a free concert going on at the Great Lawn.

The brothers skirted around it as they headed towards Columbus Avenue, and when they saw that there was no one around, Merle stopped and lit a cigarette.

Once he had it going, he looked up to find his brother staring at him.

"Yeah I know I said I quit smoking, but with all the shit going on, they help me relax."

Earl pointed behind him.

"Them cigarettes might kill you someday, but I'm more worried about him."

Merle turned, saw the big man in shadows pointing a gun at them, and the cigarette fell from his lips.

"We ain't got no money," Merle said.

Rafe Green stepped out of the shadows, his gun held at the ready.

"I don't want money. I want information, and you two are going to tell me everything you know."

CHAPTER 12 - One head is better than none

Inside Johnny R's strip club, near-naked women danced to the beat of throbbing music, while the men around them leered.

Meanwhile, amidst them sat a man lost in memory, as Joe Pullo ordered another drink and thought about Tanner.

Personally, he liked the man, and if men like him and Tanner could be said to have friends, then they were friends.

They had never gone to a ballgame or shot a round of golf, but they had worked together several times, years ago, when Pullo was an up-and-coming button man for old Sam Giacconi.

Pullo still remembered the first time he'd heard Tanner's name. That was when a snitch named Vincenzo Righettleto began wearing a wire for the Feds.

One of the whores hired for a party felt the listening device on Vincenzo as she gave him a lap dance, and later told her pimp about it. Either Vincenzo got nervous or he saw someone looking at him the wrong way, but he shot the pimp and managed to escape.

Everyone thought he would run back to the Feds and enter the Witness Protection Program, but Vincenzo was so bold that he emptied the safe of a bookmaking operation and hit the road.

He had taken off with nearly two-hundred G's in cash, and with that kind of money he could go anywhere and hide for years.

Old Sam Giacconi wanted him bad, and instead of putting a price on his head, he said that whoever hit Vincenzo could keep the money he ripped off. That was a smart move by the old man, it made everyone not only want to track Vincenzo down, but to do it as quickly as possible. The longer the thieving snitch stayed free, the more money he'd burn through, and the smaller would be the reward.

Despite the motivation, no one had a clue where to find the man. He had no family and his wife had died the year before.

A week passed, then two, but in the middle of the third week, a guy showed up at the funeral parlor Sam Giacconi owned. The guy had a white box under his arm and he insisted that he had to give it to the old man.

That's when they called Pullo.

Pullo sipped his drink and smiled as he remembered that call. It came from a punk named Al Abato. Abato told Pullo that he had a jerk at the funeral home that needed to be taught respect.

***

"Why don't you teach him yourself?"

Pullo heard a pause on the line before Abato said, "He's an asshole but he ain't no punk, you know, you can tell."

"What's his name?"

"He says his name is Tanner. You ever hear of him?"

"No, but I'll be there in ten minutes."

When Pullo arrived, he found Tanner standing outside the office doorway with a white box under his arm, and when he looked in the young man's eyes, he knew that Abato had been right in calling him. If Abato had treated Tanner as a punk, he would have been damn sorry he had.

"I'm Joe Pullo, why do you want to see Mr. Giacconi?"

"A bit of business,"

"This business, does it have anything to do with that box?"

Tanner had stared at Pullo for long moments before handing the box over.

"You'll do."

Pullo took the box, and when he eased up a corner of one flap, he saw the pale, white face of Vincenzo Righettleto staring up at him through plastic. Tanner had delivered his head in a box.

"Tell the old man that I'll be around if he needs any other work done."

Pullo stared into the box for so long that he hadn't noticed Tanner walk away, but when he caught up to him near the front doors, he called to him.

"Hey! How much was left?"

Tanner hesitated, but then answered.

"A little over a hundred grand, he used the rest to buy a boat, an old cabin cruiser."

"A boat? Hell, he could have lived on that forever."

"No one lives forever," Tanner said, and then he left Pullo holding the white box with the head inside.

***

Pullo emptied his drink and sat the glass atop the table with a sigh.

"No Tanner, no one lives forever, buddy, and it looks like your time has come."

CHAPTER 13 - Say cheese

Rafe Green was still holding the gun as he talked to Merle and Earl, but he kept it pointed downward.

The two brothers weren't the hard cases he thought they were, which was lucky for them, because if they had been a part of Pullo's crew as he first believed, he would have killed them for hurting his brother.

"Who is Tanner and why does Pullo want him dead?"

"Tanner is a hit man," Merle said. "And Pullo don't really want him dead, he'll just kill him because that's what Johnny R wants."

"Johnny R is Pullo's boss?" Rafe said.

"Yeah, if Pullo does anything it's because Johnny R told him to, but who are you? You sure ain't no Italian."

Rafe smiled, he liked the two brothers for some reason.

"Where are you boys from?"

"Earl and I travel around a lot, but we're from Arkansas, a little town called Sawyer's Creek."

"I know where it is. I used to see road signs for it when I was stationed at Fort Chaffee."

Earl and Merle broke out in huge grins.

"Hell, you're the only one we ever met who heard of Sawyer's Creek," Merle said, but then his eyes fell to the gun in Rafe's hand and he stiffened.

Rafe noticed his reaction and slid the gun into the holster on his belt.

"Tell me more about this man, Tanner."

"He's a bad dude," Earl said. "He shot Richie Sullivan this morning and says he's gonna kill Johnny R."

"Why?"

"He's crazy, that's why. He thinks he can beat an organization as big as The Conglomerate all by himself."

"The Conglomerate? I thought that was just talk, a conspiracy theory,"

"Un-uh," Earl said. "It's real, and they got more power than the Mafia ever had."

Rafe began walking while beckoning Merle and Earl to follow.

"Let's go have a beer, and you can tell me everything you know about Tanner. I think he and I may have something in common."

***

Tim Jackson stood at the curb outside the MegaZenith building, as he tried to get up the nerve to enter.

He was going undercover as part of the cleaning crew, and he would be one of over a dozen men and women assigned by the cleaning services company, *Tri-State Janitorial Services*, to clean and vacuum MegaZenith's offices, which occupied the top five floors of the building.

Tim Jackson was using the name, Tim Dyer, after he hacked into the cleaning services computer and created two false identities. He had created two identities because he thought that

Tanner would be joining him, but Tanner told him he was on his own.

Ferreting out information and breaking into others' files was Tim's forte, but Tanner assured him he would be busy using his own skills while Tim cracked open MegaZenith's computers.

Tanner's words made Tim shiver, because it meant that someone was going to die, likely many someones, but then again, if The Conglomerate was hunting for Tanner, that left them little time to search for him.

After taking a deep breath, Tim entered the lobby and walked towards the security desk. He kept telling himself that no one would recognize him, and that the MegaZenith building was the last place The Conglomerate would search for him. Tanner had said that, and he was right, at least, Tim hoped he was.

The guard at the reception desk paid him no attention as he entered, because the man was busy talking to a young woman with dark curly hair. Tim could only see the girl in profile, but it was enough to take his breath away.

Jesus, she's so beautiful.... and familiar too, where do I know her from?

The woman kept telling the guard that she was a part of the cleaning crew and that she had been assigned to clean the penthouse offices.

The guard told her that he couldn't let her up without a badge and swipe card, such as the type that Tim had forged for himself.

She's up to something, but what? If she's a corporate spy, she sucks at it.

Tim slipped back outside to wait for the woman to leave, while watching her through the glass walls of the lobby, and as he watched her argue with the guard, he remembered where he'd seen her before.

That's Frank Richards' daughter. Mallory? Melissa? Something like that, but what is she up to?

Tim had researched Richards thoroughly, because it was his computer that he was going to hack into, and the more he knew about the man, the easier it would be to break his passwords.

He took out his phone and pulled up the PDF of the notes he'd jotted down.

One child, Madison Richards, age 22,

Afterwards, he Googled her picture and saw that he was correct,

Madison emerged from the building a few minutes later, looking angry and frustrated.

Tim followed her, but then paused. If he didn't get inside soon he'd be late for his first shift.

He stood unmoving for several seconds and then chased after her.

"Madison!"

Madison Richards turned at the sound of her name, but when she saw Tim, she gazed at him in confusion.

"Hi, do I know you?"

"What were you up to in there?"

"Do you work for my father? Are you following me?"

"No. I just—"

"Stay away from me!"

Tim called out to her as she hurried away.

"I can get you inside the building."

Madison stopped walking and turned her head to look at him.

"How?"

Tim took out his phone and pointed it at her.

"Say cheese."

CHAPTER 14 - Now you see it, now you don't

Richie Sullivan dropped his phone for the second time and cursed in frustration.

His encounter with Tanner had left him without a thumb on his thickly bandaged right hand, and he was just going to have to get used to doing things with his left hand, like picking up phones, which is what he did on his third attempt to answer it.

"Hello?"

"Richie, it's Tommy, man, and I know where you can find that dude Tanner."

Richie was home at his apartment in the East Village. He was sitting on his couch in a daze of painkillers and beer, but Tommy's words roused him to full alertness.

"Where is he, Tommy? I'm going to slice off his fingers and make him eat them."

"I'm over in Brooklyn, man, at that sports bar in Greenpoint. Tanner walked in there just as bold as you please, bought a pack of cigarettes, and then left, but I followed him and I know where he's holed up."

Richie held the phone to his ear as he struggled to put on his sneakers with his thumbless hand.

"Are you sure it's him?"

"I'm ninety-nine percent sure, at least he looks like the guy in those mugshots Johnny showed us, from when Tanner did time in Mexico."

"Okay, but a lot of dudes look like those mugshots."

"I know, man, but this dude…"

"What?"

"When I looked at him, looked him in the eye… he gave me the creeps."

"That's him. I'll be there as quick as I can with Eddie, but you call the rest of the guys and have them meet us there."

"All right, but shouldn't we call Johnny R?"

"Fuck Johnny R, Tanner is mine, Johnny R can have what's left when I'm done with him."

***

Thirty-two minutes later, Richie Sullivan was looking at an abandoned apartment building in Brooklyn, which decades earlier housed scores of low-income families.

Richie studied the building, as the five members of his crew gathered around him, and thought the place might as well be on the moon for all the signs of life it showed.

The building sat surrounded by vacant lots and the remains of burnt homes. A fire swept through the neighborhood several years back on a windy day, and anything that wasn't made of brick burned to ashes.

"Are you sure he's in there? That place isn't fit to be a crack house."

"He's in there, I followed him and—look! Did you see that light on the fifth floor? That's Tanner."

Richie held a shotgun in his left hand. He gripped it clumsily with his right and chambered a shell.

"Let's go get that bastard."

They entered the building with no difficulty because the front doors were missing. They tried to be quiet, but soon gave it up. The stairs, although made of concrete, were so covered in fallen plaster and other debris that every step crunched and echoed loudly in the tomb-like building.

There was no possibility that Tanner wouldn't hear them coming, and so with Richie leading the way, they bounded up the stairs with shouts of war cries, scaring the rats, which could be seen scurrying about wherever you looked.

Richie wanted Tanner to run, with the knowledge that there was nowhere he could hide, and Richie felt invincible by the superior numbers around him.

"There he is!" Tommy said, even as Richie spotted Tanner at the other end of the fifth floor hallway, a shadowy figure dressed in jeans and a hoodie. Just about every window was devoid of glass, and the moonlight gave enough illumination to see by.

Tanner turned left, then right, seemingly a study in fear and confusion, and finally he rounded a corner and ran down another corridor.

Tanner was moving fast, but Richie and his crew ran faster, as their young legs propelled them through the decaying structure at high speed.

When Tanner passed through a doorway, they were only fifteen yards behind and shortening the divide with every second.

A door slammed to the right, the sound taking them down another corridor, and they reached the end of it just in time to see Tanner pass through another doorway, as he attempted to double back towards where the chase began.

They were twenty feet away from Tanner when Richie sent a wild blast from his sawed-off shotgun, which blew holes in a door Tanner had just slammed shut. The blast sent the door swinging open, and as they passed through it, they caught sight of Tanner just before he made a hobbling right turn.

"He's limping!" Richie cried out. "Did you see that? The bastard's limping. He must have been hit by some of the buckshot."

Had that been true, there would have also been blood, but Richie and his boys were so hyped up by the chase, that the thought Tanner could be faking an injury or laying a trap never occurred to them.

They plowed on like hounds in a fox hunt, their myopic vision focused on their weakening prey, and as they turned the corner in a single mass they found themselves running out into empty space.

***

Tanner hung from the rope he earlier secured to the side of the building and watched as Richie and his crew ran straight out into nothingness, their screams filling the night.

The screams ended when the sickening thuds began, but were followed by moans and a cry of agony. Tanner swung himself back inside and looked down at the pile of bodies, but couldn't make out any details because of the dark.

He exited the building and approached the moaning pile of broken, bleeding flesh with caution, just in case one of them was still able to use a gun.

Only two of them were still alive, a short muscular kid with greasy hair, and Richie Sullivan.

The kid with the greasy hair had broken his neck, yet still looked about with wide fear-filled eyes. The punk made no moans of pain, and Tanner suspected that he could feel nothing below his neck.

He rasped out, "No, no, please?" as Tanner placed the gun to his head, but a single bullet silenced him.

Richie had fared much better. His legs were broken, but he was straining with everything he had to squirm free from beneath the bodies of his men, and reach his shotgun, which was lying just a foot shy of his grasp.

Tanner watched Richie, saw him exhaust himself, and then waited to hear his last words.

"A trick," Richie said.

"What?"

"You... you only beat us because of a trick."

Tanner placed the tip of his gun at the center of Richie's forehead, and saw the punk's eyes cross as he looked up at the gun barrel.

"Now you see it,"

Tanner fired.

"Now you don't,"

CHAPTER 15 - New Guy vs. Old Perv

This guy is a prick and a half, Tim Jackson thought, as the supervisor of the cleaning crew glared at him.

The man's name was Carl Reese, and when Tim showed up twenty minutes late for his new job, Reese spent the next thirty minutes giving him a hard time about it.

Carl Reese was at least fifty, but dressed like a man thirty years younger, in a pair of tight black jeans and a muscle shirt. He had the arms to go with the shirt, as his biceps bulged with every gesture he made, but his lined face betrayed his age, despite the hair dye and ponytail.

"You do the toilets tonight, New Guy, and I mean every toilet, and God help you if they're not sparkling when I check them."

Reese turned his head to the left and smiled at Madison, who thanks to Tim was now going by the name of Drew Simmons. Drew Simmons was the fake ID that Tim had originally fashioned for Tanner, and it was just good luck that the name was unisex. Tim simply placed Madison's picture on the phony photo ID to make it work for her.

The three of them were standing together inside a storage room on the 57th floor that held cleaning supplies.

"You, New Girl, you'll be hanging with me tonight, it will give you a chance to meet the rest of the crew and to learn your duties."

Madison smiled.

"Whatever you say, Mr. Reese,"

"Call me Carl, honey, you and I are going to be good friends."

Tim Jackson had to bite his tongue to keep from calling Reese names. Madison was hot, no doubt about it, and he didn't blame Reese for flirting with her, even at his age, but the man was leering as if he wanted to devour her.

Tim looked at Madison, thinking that he'd see a look of disgust on her face, but no, she was smiling back at Carl Reese.

Could she possibly like the old perv?

"Hey, um, Drew, why don't we meet at break time and talk?"

Reese glared at him.

"She'll be busy, and who says you get a break?"

Tim ignored him. He and Madison hadn't talked much because they were rushed after taking the time to phony up her ID badge. Tim still had no idea why the girl was going undercover in a building her father owned, and he had taken a chance on revealing his own deception to her.

Each one knew that the other was there for some secret, if not nefarious, purpose, but Tim doubted that Madison would be killed if her real identity were known. The same couldn't be said for himself.

"We need to talk more, you know?"

Madison nodded just a bit.

"I'm sure we'll run into each other sometime, just like we did in front of the building tonight."

Tim smiled. She was telling him that she'd meet him in front of the building when their shift ended.

Reese placed an arm across Madison's shoulders and guided her out of the storage room.

"Come on, Drew, New Guy there needs to get busy cleaning the toilets."

Tim watched Madison disappear with the swarmy Reese and said a prayer that she'd keep quiet, then he pushed a cartload of cleaning supplies out into the hall, and headed for the nearest toilet.

CHAPTER 16 - It's not nice to lie

Merle and Earl had told Rafe Green everything they knew about Tanner, as they drank beer and ate Buffalo wings in a bar near Central Park.

Rafe had made it clear that he had a grudge against both Joe Pullo and Johnny R for what was done to his brother, and Merle and Earl understood where he was coming from.

They weren't big on revenge, but they could sympathize with a man seeking vengeance for a brother, since the two of them were as close as brothers could be.

After parting company with Rafe, they headed for their room, which was located in a motel that catered more to the hooker trade than actual overnight patrons. But the place was cheap, and a quick subway ride from Midtown.

They had just climbed the stairs and were three doors from their room when a man came up behind them, and for the second time that night, they were looking down the barrel of a gun.

"We ain't got no money," Merle said.

The man chuckled.

"I can believe that, you look like a couple of losers."

A car came around the corner of the building and stopped at the stairs, it was a black limo, and Johnny R's driver, Mario, got out and opened the rear door.

The man with the gun tossed his head towards the car. He had the face of a weasel with little beady eyes to match.

"Get in the car, Johnny wants to see you."

Merle was still staring at the gun. It was a big gun, a Desert Eagle.

"Who?"

"Johnny R, he wants to know what you know about Tanner."

"But we don't know—"

The man pointed the gun at Earl's face and Merle stopped talking in mid-sentence.

"Maybe he only needs one of you," the man said.

"Shit, don't shoot or anything, we'll go, no problem," Merle said.

The man lowered the gun and grinned.

"A couple of pussies, go on, get in the limo."

Merle and Earl did as they were told, and once again rued the day they met Tanner.

***

Sara watched from the rear of the parking lot as the brothers were taken away at gunpoint. The sight caused her to smile, because she was certain it meant that they had gained the attention of Johnny R.

She turned the ignition key and her car purred to life.

They would lead her to Johnny R, and sooner or later, Tanner would show, as he tried to kill the man. The Carter brothers had served their purpose. Sara wished them no harm, but cared little if harm came to them.

She cared little for anything other than finding Tanner and making him pay. She put her car in gear and followed, motivated by an obsession that would likely end with her death.

***

Johnny R stared down at the bodies of Richie Sullivan and his crew. He was looking at them from the open fifth story doorway that at one time led to a fire escape. The fire escape had rusted and fallen away after the building was condemned, and Johnny R had to admit that the drop made for a clever trap.

That is, if you were stupid.

The dumbasses, there must not have been a brain between them.

He stepped back and walked down the filthy stairs, scattering rats, until he was outside, where he stood just yards away from the corpses, and beside Joe Pullo.

Pullo asked his boss a question.

"How did you find them?"

"Eddie's girl called and said he got a call from Richie about Tanner. Someone saw him buying smokes at a bar and followed him here."

"It looks like Tanner found him. It was a trap from the word go. Hell, Tanner doesn't even smoke."

A limo parked at the curb, Mario the driver emerged, and from the rear seats followed Merle and Earl. They were led over across the debris-filled lot and stood before Johnny R, shaking noticeably in their fear, while looking sick as they stared at the bodies.

Joe Pullo smiled at them.

"Hello boys, it's good to see you again."

Johnny R sighed.

"You two aren't much to look at, but Joe tells me that you would know Tanner on sight, is that right?"

"Yes sir," Merle said, as Earl nodded in agreement.

"Joe here knows Tanner, but he won't be at my side most of the time, and from what I hear, Tanner doesn't stand out in a crowd."

"Eyes," Earl said.

Johnny R cocked his head.

"What was that?"

"Tanner's got... different eyes, intense, and kinda scary, but yeah, he looks normal other than that."

"All right, you boys will hang with me at my club, you'll be like an early warning system in case Tanner walks through the door."

Merle pointed at the pile of bodies.

"Did Tanner do that?"

"Yeah,"

"Damn."

"Yeah,"

A cry rang out from down the street.

"Get the fuck out of the car!"

Johnny R said, "Check that out," to Joe Pullo, but Pullo was already on the move, gun in hand.

The man who had grabbed Merle and Earl at their motel was shouting, and his words were directed at Sara. He had snuck up on her as she watched the gathering through binoculars, and he was aiming his gun directly at her head.

"I said get out of the damn car."

Joe Pullo aimed at her from the other side, and from his vantage point, he could see the gun resting atop the dash, beside her phone.

"Touch that gun, lady, and I'll kill you."

Sara cursed, knowing she could never shoot both of them or drive away before she'd be shot.

The other man pulled on the door.

"Unlock it, bitch!"

Tense seconds passed, and then a clicking sound came, and the man ripped the door open and yanked Sara onto the pavement.

"Easy, Vince," Pullo said, as he grabbed her purse off the passenger seat. "Bring her over to Johnny and we'll see what's what."

Merle and Earl exchanged nervous glances when they spotted Sara, but she wasn't looking at them, she was looking at Johnny R, who stared back at her with an admiring gaze.

"She's a looker, hmm boys, but unless Tanner had a sex change it isn't him, so who are you, lady?"

The man that had caught her, the weasel-faced one named Vince, read the name off the driver's license he found in her purse.

"Sara Blake, and she was carrying too, Johnny, a Glock."

"I'm a reporter," Sara said. "I work for *Street View*."

Johnny R wagged a finger in front of her.

"It's not nice to lie. I don't know what you are, but you're no reporter. You took in that pile of bodies like it was just another day at the office. Are you a cop? Maybe a Fed?"

Sara said nothing and Johnny R sighed.

"We'll take her to the club and see if anybody comes looking for her, and in the meantime, we'll give her time to think things over."

They went back to their vehicles and drove off, unaware that they had been watched the entire time they were there.

***

Tanner stepped out from behind the burnt carcass of an old Chevy van that sat atop cinder blocks.

He had recognized Sara and had no doubt that her presence there meant that she was still hunting him.

Merle and Earl's appearance surprised him, and he wondered what the brothers were up to.

Joe Pullo had been no surprise. Pullo had worked for the Giacconi Crime Family practically since birth, and he would do so until the day he died.

He thought about Johnny R and wished that he had brought a sniper rifle along, but maybe that was for the best, with any luck, Johnny R would kill Sara Blake and save him the trouble. If so, he'd better do it soon, because Tanner planned to kill him, but first, first he would deal with Joe Pullo.

Tanner walked past the bodies of Richie Sullivan and his crew, and slipped away like a shadow at dawn.

CHAPTER 17 - A hell of a way to start the day

Rafe Green sent a friendly wave towards the desk clerk at his hotel, as he headed out into the last of the night to run and clear his head.

After stretching, Rafe took off at a steady pace down West 53rd, Street. It was still dark, but dawn was lighting the eastern horizon with just the touch of a glow.

It would be a warm day, but there was a pleasant breeze and the humidity was low.

As he ran, Rafe thought about the previous day.

He had gathered good Intel from talking with Merle and Earl Carter, and he was almost certain that Joe Pullo and his crew were the men who had hurt his brother.

When he returned to Johnny R's strip club, he saw that Pullo had left, and he decided that he would return the next day and stake the place out, then, follow Pullo until he led him to the rest of his crew.

And after that?

He didn't know.

What he would like to do is kill the men for damn near killing his brother, who at last report was still in a coma.

However, Pullo was connected to The Conglomerate, an organization that Rafe had assumed was an urban legend. But the Carter brothers said that Frank Richards was a member of The Conglomerate, and Frank Richards was a key executive and large stockholder of MegaZenith, the corporation that owned the lumber mill his brother worked for, Reynolds Lumber.

And then there was Tanner, reportedly a hit man who had done work for The Conglomerate, but was now at war with them.

Tanner would be an excellent ally to have, but he might make a better patsy. If Rafe killed Pullo and his men, their deaths would be attributed to Tanner and no repercussions would befall Rafe and his family.

He could get vengeance for what was done to his brother and head back home without having to look over his shoulder.

Rafe was so lost in thought that he hadn't noticed the two figures moving in until they were almost upon him.

Pullo? His mind said, but no, he could see that the men were just a couple of young punks.

The man in front of him was black, while the one behind was white. Both men were around twenty, scruffy-looking, and carrying cheap guns.

The black man held his weapon at his side, pressed against his thigh, his finger just outside the trigger guard. Dawn was still minutes away, but this was New York City, and even at an early hour there were hordes of traffic passing by, as well as the occasional pedestrian or bike rider, and pointing a gun at someone could draw the attention of an off-duty cop.

The white man at the rear had kept his gun tucked in his waistband, but it was he and not the other man who said why they were there.

"Give us your wallet and phone, bitch."

The words had just left the man's mouth when Rafe shot his hands out, gripped the front of the black man's shirt, and pivoting, tossed the man into his partner. The two fell to the pavement in a tangle of arms and legs, and before they could recover, Rafe brought a foot down on the black man's wrist, causing him to scream and release the gun.

Meanwhile, the white man was struggling to free the gun from his waistband, but his partner had landed on top of him and trapped his arm.

When he saw that Rafe had picked up his partner's weapon, he panicked, and caused his own gun to discharge while still in his waistband.

"Oh God nooooo...." the man cried, and a red puddle formed beneath him.

His partner leapt up, his pants and shirt wet with the white man's blood, and after making an incoherent noise in his throat, he darted into the passing traffic, causing a cab to swerve wildly. Five seconds later, he was gone from sight as he ran down a side street.

Rafe looked back at the man on the ground and saw blank eyes staring up at him. The man was dead just that quick.

Dying is a hell of a way to start your day, Rafe thought.

He took a step back to avoid the spreading puddle of blood, wiped his prints off the gun he had taken from the black man, and dropped it atop the white man's body.

He then ran towards the glow in the east, and thanked God for another day.

CHAPTER 18 - Tasty

Tim Jackson smiled at Madison as she came out of the MegaZenith building, while the sun rose above the East River.

Madison returned his smile with one of her own, but Tim thought that it looked forced.

"Are you okay?"

"Yeah, but that Carl Reese gives me the creeps,"

"He didn't try anything, did he?"

"He... touched me... one of my breasts, and after that I made sure that I was never alone with him."

Tim's face darkened as his hands balled into fists.

"Wait here, I'll be right back."

Madison grabbed him by the wrist and stopped him, then, she gave Tim a bright smile.

"Reese doesn't matter, but it's very manly of you to want to protect me, especially when he's twice your size."

Tim thought about that, calmed down, and grinned back at her.

"He probably would have broken me in half, huh?"

Madison pulled him along.

"I'm hungry, let's go have breakfast."

Tim stopped short, causing Madison to stumble. Once she caught her balance, she stared back at him.

"What's wrong?"

"I… there are people after me, and if they caught me when we were together they might hurt you too."

Madison moved closer and looked into his eyes.

"Does this have something to do with my father?"

"Yeah, it does."

She took him by the hand.

"Let's go talk. I have a feeling we can help each other, and you've already helped me."

"All right, but I have a partner in this, a man named Tanner."

"Where is he, in hiding?"

Tim laughed.

"What's so funny?"

"It's just the thought of Tanner cowering somewhere."

"So you're saying he's brave?"

"I don't think Tanner feels fear, but then I'm not sure he feels anything."

***

In the Chelsea section of Manhattan, Joe Pullo walked towards his townhouse after parking his car in the lot on the corner.

He'd been awake all night and it was catching up to him. Johnny R told him to get a few hours of sleep, but he had to be back at the club by noon.

By the time he realized that Tanner was sitting on his front steps, he was only ten paces from them. Tanner's hands were empty, and so Joe stifled the reflex to reach for his weapon.

"I take it you want to talk, otherwise we'd be trading bullets."

Tanner gestured at two cups of coffee sitting in a Styrofoam holder.

"Black with two sugars, just the way you like it."

Pullo climbed the steps and sat beside Tanner. As Tanner picked up one of the cups, Pullo grabbed the other one, took a sip, and sighed with pleasure.

"That's good. You got it from the diner on the corner, didn't you?"

"Yeah, and the waitress remembered me too."

"So what's up? I doubt you came here to surrender."

Tanner turned his head and stared at him.

"I don't want to kill you, Joe."

Pullo stared back for a moment, but then broke eye contact to take another sip of coffee.

"I don't want to kill you either, Tanner, but things are what they are."

Tanner nodded.

"That's what I thought you'd say."

They sat drinking their coffee as the neighborhood stirred to life. When a blonde jogged past them with minuscule running shorts and bouncing breasts, they both followed her with their eyes.

"Tasty," Tanner said.

Joe pointed across the street.

"That one lives over there, second floor, and she likes to walk around nude with the shades up."

"Lucky you,"

"Yeah, I check her out now and then. I must have seen over a thousand girls dance at the club over the years, but I still take a peek at that one sometimes."

"It's human nature," Tanner said. "Just like the will to survive. Take a vacation, Joe, or I'll have to give you a permanent one."

Pullo tossed the remainder of his coffee into the gutter and stood, to glare down at Tanner.

"What the hell is wrong with you? You could have made a fortune with The Conglomerate, but instead you're going to war with them. Kill me, kill Johnny, and Frank Richards too, and you know what? They'll just keep coming, they're national, Tanner, hell, they're international, and they'll just keep coming until you're dead."

Tanner stared up at Pullo, whose face was red with anger, but there was concern in those eyes too.

"They wanted to own me, Joe, and no one owns me but me."

Pullo let out a huff and went to his front door.

"Leave the city, Tanner. I don't want to kill you either, but I will, goddamn it I will."

Pullo went inside and Tanner sat there for a few moments, just sipping on coffee. When he was done, he sat the cup down and walked away, passing the blonde as she made her return trip. She smiled at him and he smiled back, but there was no warmth in his smile, no warmth in his heart, for he would soon have to kill a friend.

CHAPTER 19 - Italian tube steak

At the Cabaret Strip Club, Merle and Earl yawned at the same time.

After Johnny R left them there with Vince, with orders to keep an eye on Sara, Vince took it upon himself to lock Sara into a broom closet with her hands cuffed behind her, and duct tape over her mouth, saying that he wanted to, "Soften her up,"

Vince then stared at the broom closet as he sat at the bar sipping whiskey, and thinking of Sara. After hopping off his barstool, he spoke to Merle and Earl.

"Hey, you two have any money on you?"

"I got twenty bucks hidden in my shoe," Merle admitted.

"That's enough, there's a coffee shop two blocks away, towards the tunnel, why don't you go there and bring back breakfast, I'll take ham and eggs."

Earl stood and stretched.

"We'll bring something back for the lady too."

Vince sent them a wink.

"I'll feed her while you're gone. She's going to get a nice helping of Italian tube steak, if you know what I mean."

The boys did know what he meant, and they exchanged sick glances as they thought about Vince raping Sara.

"And listen you two, don't get any ideas about running off, because then Johnny will just whack you."

"We won't run," Merle said, and as they headed for the door, Vince headed for the broom closet.

Earl opened his mouth to say something, but Merle shook his head, telling his brother to keep quiet, and then the brothers exited the club, leaving Sara alone with Vince.

***

Sara's right wrist was bleeding from her attempt to slip her hand free of the cuffs, and she was furious at herself for having been caught.

The broom closet was narrow, and the only thing she had to sit on was a plastic bucket. She was tired, hungry, frustrated, angry, and had to pee on top of it, but she was scared too, and not just for her life, because she had seen the lascivious way that Vince had stared at her.

When Vince ripped open the closet door, she blinked at the sudden light, but when she saw who stood before her, her heart rate escalated.

Vince looked her over, leering, then, he gripped her by the neck and yanked her out, causing Sara to lose her balance and fall atop the tile floor of the club's kitchen.

She kicked at him, but he stepped aside with ease, and the effort hurt, because she was lying back atop her bound hands.

She saw the first punch coming but couldn't avoid it, and Vince caught her on the chin. The second one landed at her left temple, and dazed her so much that she nearly passed out.

As she recovered, she realized that he had taken off her shoes and was pulling her jeans down. The tile floor was cold against her skin, helping to revive her, but then the knife was pressed against her throat, and she knew that she could either let him have his way, or die.

Vince saw her accept the reality and laughed at her, even as his free hand tore off the buttons on her blouse. But when he moved his hand down and slid it beneath the elastic of her underwear, anger overcame good sense and Sara bucked her hips, sending Vince off balance, causing him to slam his head against the leg of an oak table.

The knife slipped as he fell, missing her neck, but not her shoulder, and blood flowed from a long gash there.

Vince bellowed in fury.

"You fucking cunt!"

Vince was back on her in an instant, and he used his knife to slice her bra open, exposing her breasts.

Again, Sara fought, as she raised her head and bashed his sharp weasel-like nose with her skull.

Vince grunted as blood flowed down his face and his eyes unfocused, but he raised the knife high, its blade gleaming amid the fluorescent lights and chrome counters.

Sara bucked again, but it was no use, and when the knife reached its zenith, she knew that death was just an instant away.

CHAPTER 20 - Do you find me repulsive?

Tim Jackson was falling in love and he knew it.

He told Madison all about himself, about being the only child of a single mother who died when he was a senior in high school, about being a hacker, and about the price on his head. When she told him about her suspicion that her father had arranged her mother's, "accident," he felt sick inside, while wondering if Tanner had killed the woman.

But Tanner had said he didn't take those kinds of jobs and Tim believed him, he also believed that Tanner did plan to kill Madison's father.

"How much did you steal from Daddy's company?" Madison asked.

"About a million, but I did it a little at a time over a long period. I transferred it to an offshore account, and a few weeks later I learned that someone was looking for me, well, for my hacker alias, Rom Warrior."

"But now they know your real name, right? Tim Dyer."

"That's an alias too, I'm Tim Jackson."

Madison smiled.

"Hello, Tim Jackson, and aren't our lives just a mess?"

Tim reached across and took her hand.

"Not all of it,"

Madison blushed, but she also removed her hand from his.

"Sorry," Tim said. "I should have known you were already hooked up with someone, or is it that you find me repulsive?"

She giggled.

"You're cute and you know it, and, my boyfriend and I broke up last month when he moved to California."

"So… do I have a chance?"

"Let's solve our problems first, I mean you say that people tried to kill you, and what about this guy Tanner, I know you say he saved you, but he sounds dangerous too."

"Oh, he's dangerous, but he's helping me, and I think he'll help you too, but why did you want to get into your father's office? What were you hoping to find?"

"I don't know, maybe something to tie him to my mother's death. He had her killed, Tim. My dad had my mom murdered."

Tim took her hand again, and Madison let him.

"Did you find anything?"

"No. Reese wouldn't let me go in there with him. I think he's the only one who has the code for the alarm pad."

"I can bypass that."

"There's a lock too. I saw Reese remove a key from his wallet."

Tim grimaced.

"A key? Well, I'll find a way around it, and once I'm in your father's computer, I'll look for evidence that he killed your mother too."

"Why do you need to get in his office? Can't you hack into it remotely?"

"MegaZenith's firewalls are better than the Pentagon's, but everything I need is right there in your father's office."

"If that's the case, then how did you steal the money?"

"I accessed one of their subsidiary's systems. At the time, I didn't even know they were connected to MegaZenith, but um, I have to tell you something... Tanner, he plans to kill your father if they keep coming after him."

Madison looked down at the tabletop, and when she raised her head, tears leaked from her eyes.

"He killed my mom. I don't care what happens to him."

Tim heard her say the words, but he wasn't sure he believed her.

***

Outside the restaurant, Carl Reese peered through the corner of a window and watched the young couple. He had met Madison, or Drew, as he knew her, just hours earlier, but he already wanted her more than he'd wanted any woman in years.

He knew that he had no chance with her, and that she only returned his smiles because he was her boss, but there were more ways than one to get a woman in bed, and he was not above using any of them.

Carl Reese walked away before he could be spotted, as a plan for conquest formed in his mind.

CHAPTER 21 - Blood, boobs, and blushing

The knife clattered to the kitchen tiles an instant before Vince collapsed and slid onto the floor, and when Sara looked up, she saw Merle holding a fire extinguisher.

Beside him, Earl raised a fist in triumph.

"You got him a good one, Merle."

Merle grinned, but the smile faded as he saw the bloody wound on Sara's shoulder, but then his eyes drifted to her exposed breasts, and he blushed as he tore the tape from her mouth.

"You okay, lady?"

"I'll be fine, thanks to you and your brother, but please find the handcuff key before someone else comes in here."

Earl checked Vince's pockets and found it, and like his brother, he blushed at the sight of Sara's breasts.

It was one thing to ogle topless dancers on a stage who were there of their own free will, quite another to glimpse the breasts of a woman who'd been bound and nearly violated.

By the time Earl had her free of the cuffs, Merle had found a chef's jacket for Sara to put on. It was much too large for her, but it restored her modesty.

She looked at Merle and Earl with a pained expression.

"They'll kill you for helping me."

Merle pointed down at Vince.

"He sent us out for food and that's just what we're gonna do, go get food, then, we'll come back here and act like we found him."

"That could work, he did look dizzy after I head-butted him, but there's that wound on the rear of his head."

Sara looked around, found a stainless steel rolling pin, and brought it over. Afterwards, she rubbed it against the bloody laceration on the back of Vince's skull, and dropped it beside him.

"There, they'll think I hit him with that, but you two will still be taking a chance."

Merle shrugged.

"We couldn't let him hurt you, not like that, that shit ain't right."

Sara headed for the door that led to the back alley.

"Call me later at that number I gave you. I want to know that you two are safe."

She found her purse atop a shelf near the broom closet she'd been kept in, and was glad to find that her wallet and keys were in it, but her gun and phone were missing.

She turned and looked at the brothers.

"Do you know what happened to my car?"

"Yeah, they had me drive it here." Earl said, as he pointed towards the door. "It's just on the other side of that wooden fence, in the parking lot of that strip mall. I stuck your gun and phone under the seat."

"Good, thank you,"

She had opened the door when Merle called to her.

"Hey lady,"

"Call me Sara,"

"All right, Sara, we've been doing like you said, and the word is that Tanner plans to kill Johnny R and a man named Frank Richards. Richards is a big shot in The Conglomerate."

"The Chief Executive Officer of MegaZenith? That Frank Richards?"

"Don't know, but that's the name we heard."

"Good, you did well, and guys… thank you, really,"

The brothers answered in stereo.

"You're welcome,"

After Sara left by the back door, Merle and Earl left by the front, as Vince lay drooling atop the tile.

***

When Tim returned to his hotel room, he found Tanner waiting for him.

"You're late. Was there a problem?"

"Ah, well, not exactly, but I had to bring in a new partner."

Tanner stood, brought out a gun, and aimed it at Tim's midsection.

"Explain that, and it better be good."

He told Tanner about Madison, while talking quickly, his voice pitched high, and by the time he had finished, his face was damp with sweat.

"She can help us, Tanner."

"She's Richards' daughter, maybe she's setting us up."

"That's not likely at all, is it?"

"I want to meet her," Tanner said, and put the gun away.

"Just say when and where."

"Tonight, before you go to work, and about that, were you able to get into Richards' office?"

"No, hell, the asshole supervisor, a dude named Reese, he had me scrubbing toilets all night."

"Is there a chance that the girl could distract him?"

Tim let out a hoarse laugh.

"Reese has the hots for her, so yeah, she could distract him, but I mean, he might want her to do something."

"Do something?"

"Yeah, like something sexual, and I don't think she'd go that far, at least I hope not."

"It sounds like Reese isn't the only one that wants her."

"I'll get into his office, but it may take more than one or two nights to do it."

Tanner headed for the door.

"Time is not something we have a lot of, but I'll keep them busy."

"Okay, but where do you want to meet tonight?"

"I'll call later and let you know, and don't let this girl distract you."

"I won't. You can count on me, Tanner, really."

Tanner left without another word, and Tim collapsed on the bed.

***

As Madison approached her apartment, Al Trent emerged from a red Mercedes sports car and sent her a smile.

"Al? Why are you here? Did Daddy send you?"

Trent walked up to Madison and took her by the arms.

"Your father doesn't know I'm here, and I came to see you of course."

Madison brushed his hands off and sighed.

"We've talked about this, and you know that I don't feel that way about you."

"You could, in time."

"No, and I don't want to hurt your feelings, but no, and besides, I've met someone."

"Is that why you're coming home at this hour?"

"That's none of your business, but maybe you can help me. What do you know about my mother's death?"

Trent spoke wordlessly for a moment, before taking off his glasses and wiping them with his tie.

"Your mother died in an accident."

Madison squinted in suspicion at Trent.

"You know something, don't you?"

"Yes, I do know something. I know that you need to mend fences with your father, this apartment here, the lease runs out in four months, and your car will be repossessed before that. Your father has cut you off Madison, how do you expect to live?"

"I have the money grandmother left me in her will, and I can get a job as well. I don't need Daddy, Trent. I need the truth, I want to know what happened to my mother."

"She got drunk and ran her car into that gnarled tree. That's what happened."

"What?"

"I think you heard me."

"No, you said the tree was gnarled, and it is, I've seen it. I leave flowers there sometimes. But why would you go there? Have you seen photos, visited the site?"

Trent wiped his glasses again, but this time he was also sweating.

"It's just a phrase, gnarled tree, just a phrase, nothing more. Goodbye Madison."

He rushed to his car and started the engine.

Madison shouted at him through the closed passenger window.

"You know something, tell me Trent!"

The car sped off, and Madison had more questions than ever about her mother's death.

CHAPTER 22 - Comfy, but smelly

Before Merle and Earl could return from the coffee shop and pretend to find Vince, he was discovered by two members of the club's kitchen staff.

Joe Pullo was roused from bed after barely getting any sleep, and he questioned a revived Vince, as they waited for an ambulance to arrive.

"Where's the woman, Vince?"

Vince opened his mouth to lie, but when he met Pullo's gaze, he knew that it would only make things worse.

"I tried to get friendly with her."

"Don't tell me."

Vince shrugged.

"You saw her, the bitch was hot as shit. I thought I'd help myself to her while she was handcuffed. Johnny didn't say not to."

"He didn't say not to because he's not scumbag enough to think of it. She was cuffed? So how did she get away? Did you pass out when you got that lump on the side of the head there, or maybe she hit you with something?"

"Shit, Joe, I don't know, but I'll find her again, tell Johnny I'll find her."

"No. You leave her alone, and you'd better hope that she doesn't go to the cops about this."

The ambulance came and Vince was loaded aboard.

Knowing that he'd never get back to sleep, and feeling hungry, Pullo ate Vince's ham and eggs, as he sat at the bar with Merle and Earl.

"Listen up you two, Johnny usually gets in here around four, from that point on, I want you two to sit here at the bar and keep an eye on the door. If Tanner shows, raise the alarm."

"Yes sir," Merle said.

"Remember, watch the door, not the dancers, and stay sober too."

"We getting paid?" Earl said.

Pullo laughed, put down his fork, and peeled off several bills from the roll in his pocket.

"That should hold you for now, and if you want to catch some sleep before we open for the lunch crowd, there are couches in the VIP lounge where they give the lap dances, but I warn you, they smell like jism."

"Thanks Mr. Pullo, and don't worry, if we see Tanner we'll holler all right."

"Good men,"

"That woman that got away, what's gonna happen to her?"

Before Pullo could answer Merle's question, his phone rang.

As he listened to his caller, a strange look came over him. When the call ended, he turned to Merle and Earl.

"You boys might get the night off after all."

"Why's that?"

"A cabbie thinks he spotted Tanner and followed him to where he's staying."

"Are you gonna kill him?" Earl said.

Pullo stood up in a rush and knocked his stool over.

"Yes I'm going to kill him goddamnit, isn't that what they pay me to do?"

And after saying that, Pullo rushed out, leaving the brothers to wonder just what made him so angry.

CHAPTER 23 - The enemy of my enemy

As Pullo left the club, Rafe Green followed him.

He was convinced that Pullo was one of the men who had hurt his brother, and had been since talking to Merle and Earl.

But when Pullo arrived at the club in a black Hummer matching the license plate number that Robin Murphy had written down, it cinched things for him, and when he had the chance, Rafe planned to interrogate Pullo and discover who the other men in his crew were.

Joe Pullo stayed on foot after leaving the club and Rafe assumed he was headed for the subway entrance three blocks away, but when Pullo stopped in front of a coffee shop, Rafe ducked into the doorway of a boutique that had yet to open.

Pullo was only feet away and pacing in a short back and forth motion. He was so close that Rafe could hear him breathe, but unless Pullo walked in front of the boutique, neither man could see the other, because the glass enclosures that bordered the doorway were filled with displays of handbags and shoes.

At one point, Pullo muttered the word, "Stupid," and Rafe realized that the man was agitated by something.

"Joe!"

The shout came from a burly man who was crossing the street against the traffic while still tucking his shirt in his pants.

Rafe pressed himself far back into the recesses of the doorway, but the man was so busy navigating the traffic that he never spotted him.

When the man joined Pullo, he spoke in an excited tone.

"Is it Tanner? Do we really know where he is?"

"It's Tanner all right, and he's in an apartment building on East 6th. Street."

"Is he still worth fifty K?"

Pullo answered with a grunt, and Rafe thought it was further evidence that the man was upset.

The second man spoke again.

"Here's Carmine and the boys now."

An instant later, a vehicle came to a hard stop at the curb, and Rafe heard two doors open and close as the men climbed in. When the vehicle drove off, he saw that it was a blue Cadillac Escalade.

Rafe guessed that the SUV was likely stolen and would be used for the sole purpose of taking them to and from a hit. They were going after Tanner, a man that the Carter brothers had told Rafe was a paid assassin. They also told Rafe that Tanner was at war with The Conglomerate, and that meant that Tanner was going after the very people who had hurt his brother.

The enemy of my enemy is my friend. Rafe thought.

He left the cover of the doorway, walked past the curb, and hailed down a passing taxi.

CHAPTER 24 - More men than the Black Death

Rafe had the taxi driver move along East 6th Street until he spotted the blue Escalade, and then he had the cab drop him off a block past it. After that, he walked back to a deli, placed an order, and sat by the window, drinking coffee.

Joe Pullo and his men were parked near the corner of 6th Street and Avenue B, and Rafe could tell that they were staring at the apartment house on the opposite side of the street.

The apartment house was four stories tall, with a Hungarian restaurant on the ground floor, which was closed until two, and a small parking lot on its 6th Street side. There was a fire escape with its ladder raised, and the windows all had bars on them.

If Tanner made it to the roof, he could run along for only half a block before reaching the outer wall of a ten-story building that towered above its neighbors.

And other than the roof, there were only two exits. One sat to the left of the entrance to the restaurant, while the other was on the parking lot side near a row of hedges.

Both of these were in plain sight of the Caddy, and Rafe wondered why Tanner had chosen such a hiding place, one where he could be easily trapped.

***

Across the street, Joe Pullo was wondering the same thing.

He knew Tanner as well as anyone, and if there was one thing the man wasn't, it was stupid.

The hood driving the stolen Cadillac was named Carmine, and he tapped his fingers atop the steering wheel as impatience showed on his face. Carmine was the youngest member of the crew, and a gambler.

He was in the hole for five grand with his bookie, and once they bagged Tanner and claimed the reward, all his financial worries would disappear.

"What are we waiting for, Joe?"

"Are you sure he's in the front apartment on the fourth floor?"

"Yeah, I sent my girl, Angie, in there to snoop around, and the old lady on the second floor about talked her ear off. There are two apartments up there on the fourth, and the chick that lives in the front one is on vacation, while the rear one is empty because the last tenant had a fire."

"Where's Angie now?"

As if in answer to Pullo's question, Carmine's phone rang. It was Angie calling from around the corner. She confirmed that Tanner was still in the building, and Carmine told her to leave and wait for him at home.

"No one's left the building by either exit?" Pullo asked Carmine.

"No. So Tanner must still be in there."

"Angie didn't go up there though, did she?"

"Hell no, but the old woman said that there was a man staying up there who said he was vacation chick's brother, and from her description, it sounds like Tanner."

"She believed he was her brother, just like that?"

"Angie says the old woman bought the story because Tanner showed up with a family photo. The old lady said it was framed and showed the two of them as kids, real sentimental stuff."

"That part sounds like Tanner. By pretending to be the girl's brother he avoids renting a room, that's why he's been so hard to find, still, he's just about trapped up there, and that doesn't sound like Tanner."

Carmine shrugged.

"He screwed up."

"Or it's a trap."

"What trap? There are five of us. He'll never make it to the roof or the stairs and there are only a few rooms to hide in."

Pullo stifled a yawn. He had been up most of the night, and then it occurred to him that Tanner had also been awake.

He couldn't have gotten much sleep, if any, between the time he killed Richie Sullivan's crew and his appearance on Pullo's doorstep.

Tanner could even be asleep right now.

"Carmine,"

"Yeah, Joe?"

"You're with me and Frankie, while Davey takes the side exit and Christopher covers the front, but we're going in silent, dead silent, I think there's a chance that Tanner might be asleep."

Carmine chambered a round into his gun.

"If he's not asleep, he soon will be."

"Don't get cocky, Tanner's killed more men than the Black Death,"

"Bullshit, he's just a guy."

Pullo sighed.

"Yeah, just another guy to kill, that's the way to look at it."

When Pullo didn't move, Carmine opened his door.

"We're doing this, right?"

"Yeah, but we're not walking over. Drive into that parking lot, and back in on an angle so that the Caddy blocks the street view of that side door."

"You got it," Carmine said, and within seconds, they were at the building.

One man was left to guard the side door while Pullo and the others walked towards the front of the building.

And on Pullo's face was a resigned expression. The look of a man doing a job he hated.

CHAPTER 25 - A man well-versed in killing

Tanner was in a deep and dreamless sleep as Pullo and his men left the Caddy.

He had returned to the apartment on 6th Street after talking to Tim Jackson and settled in for a few hours rest.

Beside him, in easy reach, was an Atchisson assault shotgun, otherwise known as an AA-12. Tanner had a 32-shell drum magazine attached to it, and lying beside it was a bulletproof vest and a holstered gun.

He slept fully dressed and, once awakened, he could be on the move within seconds.

He had been staying in the apartment for two days but planned to move into another vacant apartment he had scouted out the day before.

He thought he was safe where he was for at least a few more hours, but he would discover that he was wrong.

***

From his position inside a nearby deli, Rafe watched as Pullo and his men drove across the street towards Tanner's hideout.

The Glock on Rafe's hip held fifteen rounds and, for a moment, he wondered if he could sneak up and cut Pullo and his crew down like dogs as they got out of their vehicle.

He immediately discarded the idea. For one thing, it was cowardly, and for another, it was likely to get him killed. He might kill three of them, possibly even four, but at least one of them would return fire before their wounds killed them.

Speaking of cowardly, it did not escape his notice that five men were sent to kill one, but then what would he expect from a group of men who nearly beat his brother to death with baseball bats.

He had to help Tanner. Had to warn his only potential ally that Pullo and his men were coming, and he had to do it in such a way that it would still leave him anonymous and off Pullo's radar.

Rafe left the deli just as Joe Pullo made it to the third floor, and then he headed towards the man guarding the side exit.

***

Joe Pullo held his breath as they neared the fourth floor apartment where Tanner lay sleeping.

He looked over at the two men with him, Carmine and Frankie. Frankie looked intense, but calm, but Carmine looked nervous, and the cockiness had left him.

Pullo whispered. "Carmine,"

"Yeah?"

"I've got point, you follow Frankie in and don't fire until I say so."

"Right Joe, and don't worry, I'm cool."

Pullo sent him a wink.

"Good man, now no talking from here on."

They moved on, slowly climbing each stair, while being careful to step to the left or the right of each tread, because the worn middle might creak, and a creaking step might warn the man they were after, a man well-versed in killing.

What should have taken just seconds, took over a minute, but at the end of that careful, cautious climb, the three men were just feet from the apartment of Ms. Claire Harper, a young woman vacationing in Mexico.

Ms. Harper would return in three days' time to find her apartment not only a crime scene, but a place of bloody slaughter.

Pullo eased closer while glancing at the door to 4B. There was yellow caution tape zigzagging across it along with red tape from the fire department which warned of, FIRE DAMAGE - DO NOT ENTER.

Pullo wrinkled his nose at the faint odor of smoke in the hall and focused again on the door of 4A.

After taking a deep breath, Pullo raised a booted foot, and readied himself to kill a friend.

CHAPTER 26 - Everybody likes a fat pickle

Davey Corelli cursed when he saw the black delivery guy headed towards him carrying a box of food from the deli. Davey was thirty, had dark-red hair, and was husky.

Damn it! This guy's got crappy timing.

Corelli was holding a Beretta and he slid it behind his back, to keep it from view.

"Yo, my man, this entrance is closed."

The black man smiled, and Davey noticed that the guy was big and looked to be in shape.

He must not eat the deli food too often, the dude is really cut,

"Closed? But I always come in this way."

"Yeah well, things change, but if you leave the food I'll make sure it gets delivered."

"It's for the guy in 2B."

"Yeah yeah, he's my cousin, now just leave the food."

"That's fine by me, but it needs to be paid for, thirty dollars."

Davey frowned, but the aroma wafting up from the food was making him drool, and he remembered that he hadn't eaten breakfast.

"What's that I smell, corned beef?"

"Hell yeah, with mustard on rye,"

"Any pickles?"

"Yeah, two big fat ones, and cannolis for dessert, the kind with the chocolate chips."

Davey's stomach overrode his brain and he slipped the gun in the waistband behind his back and took out his wallet. He opened it, lowered his eyes to look inside, and that's when the world went dark.

***

Rafe Green was smashing his gun into Davey Corelli's forehead at the same moment Pullo and his men were reaching the fourth floor.

After Davey crumbled to the ground, Rafe gazed about to see if anyone had witnessed the assault.

Out on Avenue B, the cars and people moved along, oblivious, and no one on 6th Street had seen them because the Caddy blocked the view.

Rafe dropped the box of food into a nearby dumpster, before walking back over to stare down at Davey Corelli, who had seen his face.

I have to kill him.

It was a cowardly act, killing an unconscious man, and he pushed it aside and moved into the hallway to warn Tanner.

And as Joe Pullo raised his foot to kick in the door of Apartment 4A, Rafe Green fired a shot off in the rear hallway.

***

The reverberating blast echoed throughout the building and Tanner awoke from his slumber with a start, just as Pullo kicked in the apartment door.

Tanner gripped the shotgun, but before he could even lift it from the floor, Carmine fired three shots, and death came to the apartment of the vacationing Claire Harper.

CHAPTER 27 - You're never too old for toys

Sara was watching the news when the story came on about the pile of bodies she'd seen in Brooklyn the night before.

There was speculation that the multiple homicide was the result of a gang war, and Sara chuckled without humor.

Yeah, a gang of one, and his name is Tanner.

Her paper, *Street View*, covered the story, and put forth the accusation that the killings were the work of one man who was warring against the mob. She refrained from mentioning The Conglomerate before she could gather more proof, and hoped that the story would put pressure on Tanner.

She shut off the television and leaned back in her chair. She was in her apartment on the Upper East Side, recuperating from her struggle with Vince, the would-be rapist.

The cut on her shoulder was long, but not deep, and after she treated it against infection, she bandaged it and stopped the bleeding.

The left side of her mouth still hurt from being punched, despite the painkillers she'd taken, and for some reason, she walked with a slight limp.

Vince had banged her up pretty good, and would have raped her if the Carter brothers hadn't interfered.

She had thought they were nothing more than a couple of lowlifes, but they had risked themselves to save her, and Merle had called a short while ago to say that they were in the clear.

Her phone rang and woke her just as she was about to fall asleep.

Usually, she would check the caller ID, but in her groggy state brought on by lack of sleep, and painkillers, she simply answered the call.

"Hello?"

A voice as bright as sunshine erupted in her ear, and Sara both winced and smiled, the voice belonged to her big sister, Jennifer.

"Good morning sleepy head, oh I can hear the sleep in your voice, how are you, Sara?"

"I'm fine, Jenny, and yes, I'm sleepy. I... didn't sleep well last night."

"With good cause I hope?"

"No, it wasn't that... not since Brian."

"Oh honey, I know you miss him, but Sara, you need to move on."

"Why have you called?"

"I called to talk to my little sister who I haven't seen in months. Let's get together, you sound like you need cheering up. I'll take you to FAO Schwarz."

Sara let out a loud laugh.

"A toy store? I'm not ten anymore you know?"

"I know, and I also know that I love you to death and I want to see you, so why don't we meet for lunch?"

"I love you too, Jenny, but why don't we meet for drinks tonight instead? I really do need some sleep."

"All right, baby, how about that place near your apartment that you like?"

"That's good, say eight o'clock?"

"Fine, now get some sleep."

"I will, and Jenny, thanks for calling."

"You're welcome, baby, and don't be late for those drinks, I have a ton of family gossip to tell you."

"I'll be there, bye."

Sara ended the call feeling better than she had in months.

CHAPTER 28 - A picture is worth a thousand wounds

Carmine's heart had been pounding in his chest as Pullo kicked in the door to the apartment, but he actually jumped into the air when he heard the blast of Rafe's gun echo up from the hallway.

"What was that?" he asked, and then realized that he was alone. Pullo and Frankie had already entered the apartment.

Carmine rushed in behind them, his heart beating faster than ever, and when he glimpsed movement on the left, he fired in that direction.

"Goddamn it!" Pullo shouted, and Carmine looked at his boss with shame reddening his face.

He had just destroyed a twenty-gallon fish tank, because the movement he saw was the swimming motion of tropical fish. The fish flopped on the wet carpet amid remnants of glass and colored gravel. There was fish food as well, it had been in the automatic feeder left by their owner, and the water filter vibrated on the floor, as it made a sound similar to breathing, in its attempt to clean a substance no longer there.

"It's clear back here," Frankie called, as he returned from checking out the small kitchen and bathroom. He was a lanky man with a long face and sleepy eyes.

"He's in the bedroom," Pullo said, and he and Carmine splashed across the wet carpet and towards the short hallway. There was a door on the left that turned out to be a closet, and that left the bedroom on the right.

"Tanner! It's Joe. There's no way out."

There was no answer, but there was a sound, it was the creak of floorboards.

Pullo's phone vibrated and he answered it without ever taking his eyes from the bedroom doorway.

"What?"

"Joe, it's Christopher, did you hear that shot?"

"I heard something, but I thought it was a backfire."

"Hell no, that was a shot, and it sounded like it came from in there, or maybe the side. I called Davey and he's not answering."

"Check it out, but Tanner is still up here. We hear him moving around."

"I'll check on Davey, and you guys be careful,"

Pullo put away the phone.

"We've been here too long. The old lady downstairs has probably called the cops by now."

Pullo moved towards the doorway with Frankie at his side and Carmine following. After silently counting down from three, Pullo and his men rushed into the bedroom, ready to deal death to Tanner.

***

Downstairs, Christopher ran towards Davey, who was sprawled half in and half out of the side doorway.

When Christopher caught sight of movement on the stairs, he saw Rafe and fired. Rafe fired back, missing Christopher, but hitting Davey in the chest, and killing him. The two men traded more shots, and Rafe tumbled down the stairs, wounded.

***

Joe Pullo was looking around the bedroom in bewilderment.

Tanner was nowhere in sight.

Carmine gazed up from the floor, looking equally puzzled.

"He ain't under the bed."

Frankie shrugged from the bedroom closet.

That's when Pullo noticed the picture on the wall over the bed, above the headboard. It showed a family of four standing in front of a house with a white picket fence, Mom, Dad, a boy, and a girl. It was the picture that Tanner had showed the old woman, the one he claimed was an old family photo. It was in a wooden frame and was two feet high and three feet wide.

Gunfire erupted from downstairs, as Rafe and Christopher began their battle, and the three men froze to listen, while gazing towards the hallway.

CREAK!

Pullo spun back around. The creaking sound had come from the bed, no, from behind the bed, and as he looked at the picture again, he saw an intense eye staring from a hole where the little boy's face had been.

"Tanner!"

The picture exploded as 12 gauge slugs ripped into the bedroom. However, Pullo went down first with a 9mm wound to the right side of his chest, near his shoulder, as Tanner used his left hand to fire a pistol.

Carmine received blasts from the shotgun and fell with most of his head gone, as two of the shells exited in spectacular bursts of blood and bone.

Frankie suffered a wound to his left arm and dived for the doorway, but as he stood up in the hall, six shots punctured the wallboard and two of them caught him in the hip and throat. He fell back against the opposite wall and left a streak of red as he sank to the carpet, where he would die.

Pullo was moaning from the agony of his chest wound and staring at his empty hand. He had no clue where his gun had gotten to, and with the blood leaking out of him as fast as it seemed, he guessed he no longer had a need for it.

In mild amazement, he watched Tanner crawl through the picture and drop atop the bed. The picture had been there simply to hide the hole he'd made in the wall so that he could access the other apartment, and through the hole, Pullo could make out the soot-blackened walls.

"Tricky, Tanner, you always were a tricky bastard."

Tanner grimaced at Pullo's wound and took out a phone.

"I need an ambulance," he said, and then spoke the address of the apartment.

Pullo looked down at his chest wound, as blood soaked his shirt.

"I think you should have called a hearse instead, buddy."

Tanner let out a sigh and rushed from the apartment. There were the sound of sirens in the air, and they were growing louder.

***

Knowing that Pullo ran a five-man crew, Tanner was on the alert for two more men, and when he found them lying dead at the bottom of the rear staircase, his face twisted in confusion.

"Hey, you're Tanner right?"

Tanner aimed the shotgun at Rafe, who was seated behind the wheel of the Escalade with both hands showing empty.

"Jesus! Don't shoot me, man, and get in the car. We have to get out of here."

It took Tanner less than a second to decide, and he climbed into the Cadillac. Rafe put the SUV in gear and drove away. The vehicle's glass was tinted, and he doubted anyone on the street could see inside, although there were people staring up at the building, while wondering where all the shooting sounds had come from.

"I'm Rafe Green, Tanner, and we're on the same side."

"How do you know my name?"

"I heard about you from Merle and Earl Carter."

"Those two? I thought they were with Johnny R?"

"They are and they aren't. They said they were spying on him for a woman named Sara, an ex-fed."

"I know her," Tanner said, and then he noticed the blood running down Rafe's left leg. "You're wounded, how bad is it?"

"Bad enough, but first I have to get this car off the street. I think it's stolen, and the cops are probably hearing that it left the scene back there."

"I know a place where you can get help. Head to west 26th and 10th Avenue, when you get there, you'll see a fenced in parking lot. Pull up to the gate and blow the horn."

"Is there a doctor there?"

"An illegal doctor, but she's the best, and she'll take this Caddy as payment."

"Pullo and the rest of his crew, did you kill them?"

Tanner hesitated a moment before answering.

"His men are all dead, but Pullo should survive."

"If he does, I may correct that someday."

"What's your story, Rafe Green, why the hate for Pullo?"

"He put my brother in a coma."

"If he did, it was on orders from Johnny R."

"Are you going after him next?"

"His turn will come, but I'm tired of being hunted, it's time I became the hunter."

"It's a role you're used to, isn't it?"

Tanner nodded.

"It seems I have a gift for it."

Rafe sniffed the air.

"Why do you smell like smoke?"

Tanner smiled.

"It's a long story,"

CHAPTER 29 - The one that got away

Laurel Ivy looked at Tanner with angry eyes even as her lips formed into a smile.

"Tanner. I would have thought you'd be dead by now."

"Many have tried," Tanner said, and his face was as blank as a stone.

He was at the rear of a store that sold antique furniture. The soundproofed space had its own entrance and was a doctor's office, complete with an area where operations could be performed.

Laurel Ivy, who was no longer recognized as a doctor by the AMA, still managed to have a thriving medical practice in spite of that.

She entered NYU School of Medicine with a minor cocaine habit that grew to be a major addiction by the time she was a full-fledged doctor. She was given numerous chances to get clean and went through rehab twice, but after the death of a patient was attributed to her drug use, she was kicked out of her profession.

A short time later, her dealer came to her wounded, and thus began her career as an underground doctor. The irony is, she's been clean for years, and it was her dealer who helped her, and who later became her husband.

Laurel Ivy was a blue-eyed blonde, and had paid her way through school by working as an exercise model. Although she had lived in the New York area for many years, her voice still carried a hint of her southern roots.

"Your friend will be all right, but he should stay off the leg for a while."

Tanner pulled out a wad of bills.

"How much, or is the car enough?"

"Is that all you have to say to me?"

"I thought we said everything the last time we met, Laurel."

"You don't know, do you?"

"What?"

"George died of a heart attack over a year ago, Tanner. I'm a widow now."

"No, I didn't know, and I'm sorry for you."

"That's okay, I know you never liked him."

"I liked George fine. I just liked you more."

"Despite all he did for me, I would have left him for you, but you're just not that kind of man, are you?"

"We had this conversation already."

"I know," Laurel said, and wiped a tear from the corner of her eye.

Tanner touched her on the cheek.

"We all have regrets, Laurel."

"I never regretted sleeping with you, but I'm glad George never found out."

Tanner handed her the money.

"I was never here. They want me dead."

"So I heard from Joe Pullo, he wanted to know if I'd seen you."

"Joe found me."

A pained expression crossed Laurel's face.

"Is Joe dead? Did you kill him?"

"I tried not to, but he's hurt bad."

"And what about your friend back there, Rafe?"

"They don't know about him."

Laurel took Tanner in her arms and kissed him.

"You be careful, and... you could stay at my place. They'd never find you there."

"No, but thanks,"

"They'll keep coming, Tanner, you have to find a hole and stay there."

Tanner stared at her, as memories passed through his mind. He had been with many women, but Laurel Ivy was the only one ever to haunt his dreams.

"When this is all over..."

"Yes?"

"I'll call you."

Laurel grinned.

"I'll be waiting."

CHAPTER 30 - The canary

Al Trent entered Johnny R's club, and when he saw Merle and Earl seated at the bar, he walked over.

"The place ain't open yet, mister," Merle said.

"I'm here to see Johnny R."

Carl the bartender spoke up.

"Johnny said to send you back to his office, Mr. Trent, it's right down that hallway."

Trent sent Carl a nod of thanks and headed towards the office.

Merle watched him walk away and then spoke to the bartender.

"Who's he? I got boots older than him."

Carl laughed.

"He's some boy genius, the corporate type. I'll tell you, fellas, it sure ain't like the old days when Sam Giacconi ran things. A college boy like that would have been laughed out of here, now he's giving orders."

"Him?" Earl said in shock.

"That's Frank Richards' right hand man, and I bet he's here to talk about Tanner."

"Any news on Joe Pullo?" Merle asked.

"The word is he'll live, but he's out of the fight, and the rest of his crew is dead. I know you boys are here to help me keep an eye out for Tanner, but I'll tell you a secret, if he comes in that door again, I'm not warning anybody, I'm just hitting the deck."

"Tanner wouldn't come here, would he?"

"All I know is that I'm glad I'm not Johnny, because I think he's Tanner's next target."

***

Inside the office, Johnny R was shouting into Al Trent's face.

"I want Tanner! That bastard wiped out my best crew."

Trent remained calm and spoke in a normal voice.

"Mr. Richards is determined to see Tanner dead, so much so, that he's raised the bounty to one-hundred thousand."

"Hell, for that kind of money I may hunt him down myself."

"There's news about that woman, Sara Blake,"

"What news, did she go to the cops?"

"No, and she is a reporter of sorts. She recently acquired a half interest in *Street View*. She's also an ex-FBI agent who left under a cloud, but we don't know what that might be, however, it concerned Tanner, apparently, she despises the man."

"Huh? Now that's interesting,"

"If you see her again, pick her brain, she might know something that can help us find Tanner."

"Maybe, but I still think Tanner will show here."

"In that case, I think I'll leave."

Trent headed for the door and Johnny called to him just as he opened it.

"I want you to remind your boss of something. If Tanner kills me, he's next."

Trent smiled.

"That would make you the canary in the coal mine, and we know what happens to them. Goodbye, Mr. Rossetti."

Trent closed the door, and Johnny R stared at it, while fighting the urge to run after Trent and place a bullet in his head.

CHAPTER 31 - Cute, but scary

Tim Jackson swallowed hard as Tanner climbed into the rear of Madison's BMW. They were meeting at Liberty State Park in Jersey City, New Jersey, and the Statue of Liberty loomed large in the foreground as the last rays of sun melted away.

Tim was in the passenger seat, but Tanner was in the back with Madison, and he stared at her as if trying to read her mind.

"Hello?" Madison said, and her voice sounded shaky.

"Why do you think your father had your mother killed?"

"She, she was going to leave him. Daddy married her when she was younger than I am, but she wanted her freedom and threatened to divorce him."

"What did the cops say?"

"They said it was an accident, but I know he killed her, had someone kill her, because I saw it in his eyes."

Madison fought back tears as she ran a hand through her dark curls. Tim reached back over the seat, and she took his hand.

Tanner noticed the look of affection Madison gave Tim as she squeezed his hand, and thought it seemed genuine.

"Your father wants me dead, but I'm going to kill him first, so proving him guilty won't matter. He won't be living long enough to go to jail."

A look passed between Tim and Madison, and then Tim asked a question.

"That pile of bodies they found, was that you?"

"Yes, that was Richie Sullivan and his crew."

"And this morning, those men downtown?"

"That was me as well, but I had help there, and that was just the beginning. The Conglomerate has declared war on me, and I'm going to make them sorry they did."

"Thank God I'm on your good side, and I will get into Richards' office. Madison and I have a plan."

"The sooner the better, but be careful. The Conglomerate doesn't play games, if you're caught, you'll be killed."

"Tanner," Madison said, and when Tanner looked at her, he saw she looked anxious.

"What is it?"

"You, you didn't kill my mother, did you?"

"No. I don't do that sort of work, and if I had to guess, your father gave the job to someone he knew he could trust, probably an amateur. If Johnny R knew about it, he could use it for blackmail, your father would know that."

Madison looked as if a light had just come on in her mind.

"Al Trent, it was Al Trent. He's Daddy's assistant, and he worships Daddy."

"It's possible," Tanner said.

"Were you going to kill him too?"

"Only if he got in my way,"

Madison sat up straighter, as mixed emotions danced across her face.

"I don't give a damn about Al, but his Sister Marci and I were best friends all through high school, and his mother's a sweetheart too. If he died, it would destroy them."

"He should pay for killing your mother," Tim said.

"You're damn right he should, and maybe we'll find proof in my father's files that will put him away for it."

"That's not very likely," Tanner said. "But I'll try to come up with a plan that will make him accountable for your mother's death. It will be payment for you helping Tim, but understand something, this doesn't end until we get The Conglomerate's files and break their encryption. That's when we'll be able to blackmail them."

"I've been working on that," Tim said. "And once we get the records, we'll leave New York."

"And go where?" Tanner said.

"I've got a place, a farm near the New Jersey/Pennsylvania border with lots of land, it's where I was headed when I was forced to hide in that warehouse."

"I hope it's safe and untraceable."

"It is, and remote as hell."

Tanner stared at him.

"Get those files. I'm good, and I'm hard to kill, but everyone's luck runs out, and I'm going to push mine to the limit."

"You can count on me, Tanner, you can count on us. Madison is going to run interference while I break into her father's office."

Tanner climbed out of the car.

"This night supervisor, Carl Reese? Don't underestimate him."

"We won't, and Tanner, stay safe, man."

Tanner nodded at both of them, went to his vehicle, and drove off.

Madison joined Tim in the front seat and let out a long breath.

"That was a little scary, but I think I like him, and I didn't expect him to be so hot."

Tim opened his mouth in shock.

"Tanner?"

"He's cute, scary, but cute,"

"And what about me?"

Madison reached over and took Tim in her arms. After a long kiss, they parted, but Tim wrapped his arms around her as Madison leaned back against him.

"Tim, I'm scared, are you sure that drugging Reese will work?"

"Yeah, but remember, you have to drug him after he opens up your father's office."

"I know, but I worry about being alone with him. He really is a pig."

"Be nice to him for one more night and we'll be home free."

"And Tanner?"

"Tanner won't stop until he kills everyone that wants him dead."

"Like my father,"

"Yes."

Madison grew quiet, as tears rolled down her cheeks.

CHAPTER 32 - I know just the guys

In a midtown pub, Sara greeted her sister Jennifer with a kiss and a hug.

The two sisters looked much alike, but Jennifer was a natural blond and her eyes were an ice blue. She was six years older than Sara, had been married briefly, and ran a nonprofit that helped to fund clinics in third world countries.

Sara was not alone. She was seated at the bar with a burly man of fifty whose nose had obviously been broken many times. Before her sister arrived, Sara had passed the man an envelope. The envelope held money, money for a certain... service.

"You understand what I want done, correct?"

The man smiled. It was not a pleasant smile.

"Don't worry, I know just the guys."

"How soon will it happen?"

"As soon as possible,"

"Thank you, Duke, and good night,"

"Goodbye ladies."

The man walked off and Jennifer pointed after him.

"Who was that?"

"Just an old acquaintance from my days with the Bureau,"

"You were rude. You forgot to introduce us."

"No I didn't, and you're early."

Jennifer kissed her on the cheek again.

"I'm early because I couldn't wait to see you, and have you eaten dinner yet?"

"No, actually I've eaten very little and I'm hungry."

Jennifer smiled.

"We'll get a table."

Sara had slept most of the day and awoke feeling better, but her mouth was still sore from Vince's punch, and so she ordered a pasta dish.

* * *

They spoke of family during the meal, but as they considered what to have for dessert, Jennifer asked Sara about herself.

"Do you miss being an FBI agent?"

"Some, but I think the newspaper will keep me busy."

"I'm surprised you don't want to practice law like Daddy."

"I think that would bore me to death."

"You never did say why you were fired."

"I don't want to talk about that. Why don't we just have a pleasant evening."

"Are you dating anyone?"

"No… I'm still not ready for that."

"I didn't know Brian well, since I only met him once, but I could tell that he loved you, and I think he would want you to move on."

"Maybe someday, but what about you? Are you seeing anyone?"

"I was dating a co-worker for a while, but he took a job in Washington DC, and I didn't want a long-distance relationship."

A few seconds later, Jennifer gasped in the middle of a sentence, as she stared over at the bar.

"Oh my God, that is one handsome man, and he's looking this way."

Sara turned her head to the left and saw her old partner staring at her, FBI Special Agent Jake Garner.

CHAPTER 33 - No lube

Seven blocks west of the pub where Sara was dining with her sister, there was a restaurant named *Jangles*, which was owned and frequented by members of The Conglomerate.

Dante Celso stepped out of his limo in front of the eatery, and was headed towards the front door with two bodyguards flanking him.

Dante was a cousin of Johnny R, and the man who ran The Conglomerate's massage parlors.

He was aware of Tanner, and knew that the man had caused havoc and made threats against his cousin and others, but he thought that it had nothing to do with him.

He was wrong.

Dante Celso's dead body was falling towards the ground even as the shot that killed him echoed among the city's concrete canyons, signaling the beginning of Tanner's terror spree, by morning, there wouldn't be a Conglomerate member in the city that felt safe.

***

Rafe Green returned to his hotel room and limped over to the bed.

He'd been wounded twice while in the army, and illegal or not, Laurel Ivy was a good doctor. The stitches she put in his leg were sewn tight, and whatever she'd given him for the pain was working, because his leg wound felt pleasantly numb.

After a shower, he ordered room service, and then just sat on the side of the bed reliving the events of the day. He had killed two of the men that had attacked his brother, and the other three were either dead or injured.

Joe Pullo was still alive, and Tanner had asked Rafe to let him be, with the promise that he would deal with Pullo's boss, Johnny R.

Rafe had agreed, grudgingly, but if his brother died—his cell phone rang.

When he looked at the caller ID, he felt apprehensive. It was his sister calling. Had Jerome passed away?

After taking a deep breath, Rafe answered.

"Hey Debby… is there news?"

"He's awake! Jerome is awake and he seems fine, oh Rafe, Jerome is back!"

Rafe let out a laugh of relief and wiped at tears of joy, the pain, stress, and horror of the day forgotten.

***

Sara frowned as she watched her sister touch Jake Garner once again.

The handsome FBI agent had charmed Jennifer within moments of meeting her, and the three of them had been chatting for some time, through dessert, and several drinks.

Despite having once shot him, Sara liked Garner, but he was the last man she would want her sister to get involved with, because Jennifer wasn't frivolous when it came to love, while Garner was a world-class lothario.

"Didn't you say you had to work tomorrow, Jenny?" Sara said.

Jennifer sent her sister a wink.

"You don't fool me, Sara, you want Jake all to yourself, but you're right, I do have to get up early, and so I'll say goodnight."

"You didn't drive here, did you?"

"No honey, don't worry, I'm taking a cab, and you do the same. You drank as much as I did."

Garner rose as her sister stood, and Jennifer gave him a peck on the cheek.

"I hope to see you again, Jake."

"I would like that as well," Garner said.

Sara gave her sister a kiss and a hug goodbye, and after Jennifer departed, she stared at Garner.

"No."

"No what?"

"Not my sister. She's not going to be one of your conquests."

"That would be up to her, wouldn't it?"

"There are plenty of other women in this city, or have you already had them all? At the rate you go through women, I wouldn't be surprised."

Garner laughed, but then his face turned serious, and he reached over and took Sara's hand.

"How are you? I mean how are you really?"

"I haven't given up on finding Tanner if that's what you mean."

He released her hand and touched her cheek tenderly.

"Does that bruise have something to do with Tanner?"

Sara looked surprise and took out a makeup compact to check her face in the mirror.

"I didn't think it was noticeable, Jenny never mentioned it."

"Jenny isn't a trained observer, but I am, and you haven't answered my question."

"Yes, it did have something to do with Tanner, although it wasn't caused by him."

Garner stared at her while shaking his head.

"I wish you could let Tanner go, but live and let live just isn't part of your DNA, is it?"

Sara smiled, and it was a smile much like the one on the face of the man she'd been meeting with when her sister showed. A smile devoid of all warmth,

"I don't do forgive and forget, a fact the man who gave me this bruise will learn the hard way."

***

On Mulberry Street, Vince Maggio, Sara's would-be rapist, awoke with a start, as a gag was shoved into his mouth and secured with a length of duct tape.

When he tried to sit up, two sets of powerful hands pushed him to lay flat atop his bed, before flipping him over to secure his wrists behind his back.

His boxer shorts were yanked off, leaving him naked, then, his ankles were spread and secured by coarse rope, while pillows were wedged beneath his midsection, causing his ass to rise, and become more accessible.

Vince bellowed behind the tape, but the pleas and protests came out unintelligible and would not carry beyond the walls of his apartment.

As one man held him down, the other stepped out of his pants, and soon he was positioned on the bed behind Vince, Vince who was shedding tears born of dread.

The man smacked Vince hard on the ass, and began screwing the top off a tube.

The second man spoke up. He was smaller than the first man, even though he was six-foot-four and weighed three-hundred pounds, however, their anatomy would be only one of Vince's concerns, they also brought along… toys, extra-wide, extra-long… toys.

"No lube, man, Duke said the lady wants it to hurt."

The other man shrugged, took aim, and gave Vince cause to scream.

From that night forward, even hearing the word rape made Vince Maggio want to vomit.

CHAPTER 34 - Stone cold sober

Tanner killed two men inside a Conglomerate drug warehouse before the other bodyguards could pinpoint where the shooting was coming from.

He then used one man as a shield, as he tossed an incendiary grenade beneath a long table where money was stacked high.

The grenade was a dud Tanner had rigged, but it smoked and sizzled and caused everyone to head for the exits, including the bodyguards, who shoved and trampled their unarmed co-workers who were there to count the money.

Tanner found himself alone within seconds and used an arm to swipe piles of cash into a knapsack, while wincing at the pain in his side. He'd been hit in the vest, and the rib beneath it hurt like hell.

With the sack full of cash, he tossed a live grenade beside the dud he had thrown. This grenade was also specially rigged, with a longer than normal fuse.

Tanner went neither to the front nor the back, but to the roof, where he had earlier killed the two guards positioned there.

As he stepped out into the night, he could hear the bodyguards rushing back into the room, some cursing vehemently at having been deceived.

Tanner closed the door to the roof behind him just as a blast emanated from below, followed by the screams of his enemies.

The Conglomerate, in the person of Frank Richards, declared war on Tanner, and Tanner was waging war in return.

Within seconds, he was four roofs away and climbing back down a rope he had used to climb up, and then he was driving away in the vehicle of a bookie he had killed earlier, his night of death not yet done.

***

Sara wondered where the time went to, as she and Garner left the pub at closing time, which was two a.m., when he mentioned that he knew a nearby jazz club that stayed open until four, she gave him a sly smile.

"Are you trying to get me drunk?"

"I think we're both nearly there, but I really just want the night to continue. I enjoy your company, Sara."

Sara laid a hand on his cheek.

"I had a good time too, Jake. You're more interesting than I would have thought, but, I think I should be getting home."

"I'll escort you."

Sara opened her mouth to say no, but as she looked up into Garner's face, she uttered the word, "Fine,"

They were standing before her apartment door a short time later, and Sara could feel the alcohol seeping into her bloodstream. She realized that she hadn't been drunk in a long time, and couldn't remember the last time she had enjoyed an evening out.

Garner bent to kiss her, but she pressed a hand against his chest and wouldn't let it happen.

"I'm not inviting you in. I like you, and you're every bit as good looking as you think you are, but I'll be damned if I'll be just another conquest for you to brag about."

Garner looked abashed and took a step backwards, and to Sara's surprise, she felt disappointment over him giving up so easily.

Her resolve was weakening. She hadn't been with a man since Brian Ames, and like most young women, she had her needs.

Garner gazed into her eyes.

"I'm sorry, I shouldn't have done that. You've made your feelings about me plain, and I should respect that."

"I don't dislike you, Jake, in fact, the more I see of you, the more I like."

"Then, may I see you again?"

She blinked in surprise.

"What? You mean like a date?"

"On any terms you want, but I'd like to stay in contact."

Suspicion seeped into her gaze.

"You accused me earlier of holding a grudge, but what about you? After all, Jake, I did shoot you once."

"Actually, you shot me three times, and I don't hold that against you, well, not much anyway. You have my number, and… I hope to hear from you."

He kissed her, but it was just a quick peck on the cheek, and then he was walking off towards the elevator.

Sara watched him go as mixed emotions roiled within her, and she nearly called him back.

After Garner disappeared onto the elevator with a wave goodbye, Sara fumbled with her keys and entered her apartment.

She hit the light switch even as she closed the door, and when she turned around, she saw Tanner standing in her living room and pointing a shotgun at her.

The sight sobered her instantly.

CHAPTER 35 - Mama's boy

Tim Jackson could hardly believe his luck as he slid in behind Frank Richards' desk at MegaZenith.

He and Madison had come up with a plan to drug Carl Reese by putting the date rape drug, Rohypnol, in Reese's coffee at break time, and had bought several of the pills from a pot dealer in the East Village.

The plan proved to be unnecessary, because after entering the security code and unlocking the door, Reese was called away to deal with a crisis of some sort on a lower floor, and failed to secure the office when he left.

Madison, who had been watching Reese, alerted Tim of their opportunity, and as she kept watch for Reese's return, Tim attempted to plunder Richards' computer files.

After powering the computer on, a sign-up screen appeared and asked for a password.

Tim had questioned Madison extensively about her father's life in an attempt to guess what he would use as a password. The likelihood that he could access the computer on site was almost nil, given the constraints of time, but with Madison's intimate knowledge of the man, he hoped to do so.

If he could download Richards' files and leave the computer intact, it would give him and Tanner a huge advantage, in that they could possibly gain access to The Conglomerate's network without their being aware. But if Tim had to take the hard drive with him, it would alert them within hours.

Madison seemed certain that her father's password would have something to do with her late grandmother, a woman her father worshiped, but who Madison never cared for much, because her grandmother didn't like Madison's mother, and let her feelings be known at every opportunity.

After wiping his damp palms on his jeans, Tim typed in the name of Richards' late mother, Christine.

The computer beeped, informed him that his input was wrong, and reminded him that he had only two more chances to enter the correct answer, or be locked out.

Madison stuck her head in the door and Tim looked up with a start, thinking her appearance meant that Reese was on his way back.

Madison smiled.

"Any luck?"

"Her name didn't do it, and if I had any sense I would just rip out the damn hard drive and get the hell out of here with it. The odds of me guessing right are astronomical, even with your help. He could just be using a random alpha-numeric sequence of some sort, the password doesn't have to have any meaning to him at all."

Madison shook her head in disagreement.

"Daddy likes to keep things simple. It's why he always has an assistant like Al Trent at his side. He lets them worry about the details and minutiae. The password would be simple, I know it."

Tim ran a hand through his hair.

"All right, I'll try again, but please go back and watch the elevator. We don't need Reese finding us in here, and what's that bag in your hand, garbage?"

"I emptied the shredder."

"Why? Anything in there would be in a thousand pieces."

"I've always been good with puzzles, now get back to work."

Madison threw him a kiss and returned to the hallway.

Tim watched her go, stared at the screen and typed in the name of Frank Richards' childhood pet, a pug named Sparky, who Madison said Richards had mentioned often over the years.

WRONG ANSWER - ONE ATTEMPT REMAINING

Tim stood, walked around the desk once, and sat back down to take his last shot.

It's the mother. Madison says her father is a mama's boy, so it has to be the mother.

Tim typed in the name that Frank Richards called his mother until the day she died.

MUMSY

The sign on screen disappeared and the desktop came up, bringing with it a background picture that shocked Tim.

It was a picture of Madison, or at least it would be if she were fifty years older. The background picture was a photo of Frank Richards' mother, a woman who must have looked remarkably like Madison in her youth.

Tim muttered, "Mumsy? What a mama's boy," and then he went to work draining every shred of data from Richards' computer.

CHAPTER 36 - No justice, no peace

Sara and Tanner stared at each other for ten seconds before Sara broke the silence.

"I'm still breathing, so either you want to talk, or you're waiting for me to beg for my life. If it's begging you want, you'll be disappointed."

"Place your purse on the table and walk over here," Tanner said.

Sara did as he said. Her gun was in her purse, but she knew it might as well have been absent for all the good it would do her.

After walking into the living room, she stood ten feet from him, and felt the tension drain from her shoulders when he lowered the shotgun.

Tanner was dressed in black from head to toe and still wore the bulletproof vest, which had been marked by slugs in several places. The long-sleeved shirt beneath it had a hood attached, and it hung down his back like a mane, while behind him, on an arm of the sofa, was a trench coat and hat.

"There's blood splatter on your clothes, been working late?"

"I watched Johnny R's men capture you last night, and yet here you are, safe and sound, does that mean you've joined The Conglomerate?"

Sara searched Tanner's face for deception.

"Brian said that The Conglomerate was more myth than truth, and that the corporate side was being used by the mob."

"That may have been true at one point, but it's more like the reverse now. Frank Richards runs The Conglomerate in New York, and he's also the man who ordered Brian Ames death."

"The CEO of MegaZenith? I heard that before and found it hard to believe, but why are you asking me about this?"

"Curiosity, how did you get away from Johnny R?"

"I had help, those two brothers,"

"Merle and Earl Carter?"

"They were helping me to find you."

"So that you could kill me?"

"Yes."

"You've found me."

Sara said nothing and the two of them stared at each other again. This time it was Tanner who broke the silence.

"I don't want to kill you, but I will if you keep coming."

Sara moved towards Tanner until she was standing before him, screaming up into his face.

"You might as well kill me now you son of a bitch, because if it's the last thing I do I will see you dead!"

Tanner moved the shotgun between them and placed the barrel under Sara's chin, pushing her head back even more. Her gaze never wavered, but she trembled.

They stood like that until Sara felt the muscles in her neck cramp from the pressure, and then the shotgun moved away, only to come crashing down on the side of her head.

Sara moaned once, dropped to the floor as if devoid of bones, and rolled onto her back.

Tanner gazed down at her with cold eyes, not seeing a beautiful woman, but an enemy.

"You've been warned."

CHAPTER 37 - So they keep telling me

With Joe Pullo's crew gone, Johnny R was forced to go to his bench.

However, Gino Tonti was no minor leaguer, but rather a man who had been Sam Giacconi's enforcer.

Tonti was sixty-eight, still fit, and had been in charge of placing men to act as bodyguards at the various drug dens, massage parlors, and gambling establishments. Gino Tonti was also the man who mentored Joe Pullo.

Although Gino hadn't pulled the trigger on anyone in over twenty years, he had killed many in his youth. He also knew Tanner on sight, and after handpicking six of his best men, he was determined to track Tanner down and kill him.

They assembled in a machine shop in the Bowery that Gino owned, and that also manufactured cheap guns and homemade silencers on the side.

Gino looked at the six young men before him and wondered what they were feeding kids nowadays. The six all stood a head taller than Gino and were wide as linebackers.

Like Tanner, they were dressed all in black and wore vests. Each man carried a semi-automatic pistol and spare clips, and three of them had spent time in military war zones and lived to tell about it.

They weren't afraid of Tanner, they were eager to bag him, because they knew that by doing so, their stock would rise within The Conglomerate.

"All right, you all have the new cell phones I gave you and here's how we'll play it. I'll take Tony and Mike and work midtown, while Al and Brenner stay in this area, Marzo and Bobby will head uptown, and the second we get a sighting of the bastard, whoever's closest tracks him down while the rest of us converge."

One of the men spoke up. He was Tony, a handsome man with a cleft chin, and Gino had known him since he was a boy.

"Where was he spotted last, Gino?"

"The upper east side, but a pimp was knifed near Times Square. The pimp is still alive, so I don't think it was Tanner."

While running a hand over his thick white hair, Gino gazed from face to face, and saw a look of fierce determination on each man.

"Tanner thinks he's invincible, but he's wrong, and by morning we'll be bringing Johnny his head."

The men cheered loudly and patted each other as if they were about to play a rugby match. They were ready, pumped, and eager to kill.

They filed out into the parking lot and were headed for their cars, keys in hand, when a shadow to their left moved.

***

Tanner opened up with the Atchisson assault rifle, killing the first two men with head shots, while knocking another on his back with a hit to the chest.

The remaining men fired back, but Tanner was positioned behind an industrial dumpster heavy with metal scraps, and their shots weren't making it through to the other side.

Two more men died, but then Gino dropped to the ground and fired round after round into the cinder block Tanner stood on, causing it to crumble. Tanner fell sideways, to lay atop the parking lot, and nearly lost his grip on the shotgun.

Gino fired a shot at Tanner's face, before needing to reload, but it missed and ricochet off one of the dumpster's iron casters.

Tanner rolled to his left, as the remaining two men joined Gino down on their bellies, and Tanner let loose with a volley of five shots, wounding Gino, killing Tony, but missing the third man. However, blood splatter from Tony's wound blinded the man temporarily, giving Tanner time to move again.

The man swiped the blood from his eyes, even as he fired blindly at the place where Tanner had been. The shotgun empty, Tanner removed a Glock from a side holster and killed the man with three shots.

Gino's weapon went flying away when Tanner wounded him in the right arm, severely injuring the limb below the elbow, but Gino still had a knife in an ankle holster, and he tossed it with his left, while saying a prayer.

Tanner grunted in pain as the knife embedded itself in his thigh. It was in over an inch deep and quivering like an arrow. It could have been worse. Gino had been aiming for his throat.

Tanner stood, pulled the knife free, and felt a warm, wet stickiness flow its way down and into his boot. He picked up the shotgun and limped over to stare down at Gino.

"I figured Johnny would call on you, Gino."

"I should have stayed out of it at my age, but he's the boss."

"That's a nasty wound," Tanner said.

He tucked the shotgun under one arm and took off his belt, then secured it tight around Gino's upper arm.

"Keep pressure on that or you'll bleed to death."

Tanner walked past him, the limp noticeable, but minor, and Gino called to him.

"You'll never win this, Tanner, it's just a matter of time."

"So everyone keeps telling me," Tanner said, and then he scooped up a set of keys from the ground, and drove off in Tony's ride.

CHAPTER 38 - Half a homo and a sweet piece

Tim finished erasing any sign that he had accessed Richards' computer and joined Madison in the hallway.

When she spotted him, she raised her eyebrows in inquiry.

"Did you get in?"

"I did, and I got everything. It's all here on a data stick and I also sent it to a cloud storage site, now comes the hard part. I have to break the encryption."

Madison grabbed him and kissed him on the lips.

"You'll do it, I have faith in you."

"Thanks, but it'll take a miracle. I tried to explain that to Tanner, but he wouldn't listen."

"So what do we do now, sneak out?"

"No, let's finish our shifts, and in the morning we'll tell Reese that we decided to quit. I think if we just left all of a sudden it might raise suspicion."

When they stepped on the elevator, Tim placed his foot against the door so that it wouldn't slide shut.

"Do your thing," he told Madison.

Madison made a call. Downstairs in the security office, the phone rang and a male voice answered.

"Security,"

"Hi, I was looking for Mr. Reese, is he there?"

"No, he's not."

"Okay, sorry to bother you."

"No problem."

While Madison talked to the security guard, Tim shut down the automatic loop that showed the corridor outside Richards' office to be empty. If the guard had been looking at the monitor for that camera, he might notice a slight gap in the picture, but by Madison calling, Tim hoped it would distract him.

The feed on the camera went back to normal just as the door closed on the elevator, and inside the ground floor security office, the guard noticed nothing amiss.

Madison stayed on the elevator to ride to a lower floor, while Tim got off and headed to a supply closet. He would gladly scrub toilets until it was time to leave, knowing he would never have to see the place again, or Carl Reese.

Just as he thought of the man, Reese appeared.

"Dyer, how are those shitters coming?"

"I've still got an entire floor left, but I'll get it done."

"Make sure you do, and while you're doing that, I'm going to supervise the new girl."

"She's got a name, you know?"

"She's got a great ass too," Reese said, and slapped Tim on the shoulder, causing it to go numb.

Tim grimaced, rubbed at the ache, and headed for the freight elevator with fresh supplies.

***

Carl Reese watched Tim go and then made his way to his tiny office, which was actually a converted storage closet.

After settling behind his desk, he thought about Tim, and smiled.

He had discovered that Tim and Madison were phonies only by a fluke of luck. He'd been called to the corporate headquarters of the cleaning services company he worked for, which was located in Southern New Jersey, for of all things, mandatory sensitivity training.

He hadn't been singled out, but was one of a group of supervisors. He resented it all the same, and thought the training was a bunch of bullshit.

After sitting through a film and taking a quiz, he talked to a friend who worked in the personnel office.

When he mentioned Madison, who he knew as Drew, his friend, a man named Eric, looked blank.

"We haven't hired any newbies in weeks."

"What do you mean? There are two of them, a half a homo named Tim and a sweet piece of ass named Drew," Reese said, thus revealing that the sensitivity training had no effect whatsoever on him.

When Eric checked the computer, they found the records that Tim had placed in their system.

"Here they are, but how? I process all of the new hire paperwork for the entire company, and I never did this."

Reese smiled.

"You've been hacked."

Eric scratched his head.

"I guess, but who would hack into our system so that they could get a job scrubbing toilets?"

"Corporate spies, that's who. They don't give a shit about us, they're after something at MegaZenith. Listen, keep this to yourself, there's money here somewhere, and I'm going to get a piece of it."

Eric agreed, for a piece of the action, and Reese returned to the city.

Tim and Madison had been planning to drug Reese, but little had Madison suspected that Reese had the same fate planned for her. He was going to slip her something at break time, play the concerned supervisor and escort her home, and then have his way with her, but the scent of money derailed that plan.

Reese sat his feet up on a corner of his desk and wondered just what it was that Tim had stolen from Frank Richards' computer.

Whatever it was, it would soon be his to take.

CHAPTER 39 - The guy from *Die Hard?*

Sara awoke on her living room floor just before daylight.

Her head ached, and when she tried to stand, she vomited.

She finally stood, only to fall onto her sofa, and when she touched the side of her face, she felt dried blood, which had run from a wound beneath her scalp.

Tanner. Why didn't he kill me?

She stood once again and the room swam before her eyes, but she made it to the table by the door, where she'd left her purse.

The thought occurred to her that she should check her apartment and be certain that Tanner left, but she knew he had gone, and besides, it was an effort just to make it back to the sofa.

"I have a concussion," she murmured to herself, and realized she needed to see a doctor.

Once she had her phone in hand, she called for an ambulance.

"You fucked up, Tanner. You should have killed me when you had the chance."

***

Merle and Earl both startled awake from the pounding on the door of their motel room.

The brothers had only been asleep for a short while, after spending all night at the club, watching the door for Tanner.

"Shit, who's that?" Merle called.

"It's Mario, guys, Johnny R's driver. Johnny wants you two back at the club right now."

Merle crawled out of his bed as Earl sat up in the other one. When Merle opened the door, Mario grinned at him. He was a fat man, forty-one, with a handlebar moustache.

"All hell broke loose last night, boys, and it's all hands on deck. You got five minutes to get ready and then we're going to the club."

Earl came over to the door while scratching his privates.

"What happened? Tanner?"

"What else? Johnny's ready to go ballistic. He's also called an early morning meet-up with some Conglomerate dude. I think they're gonna pull out all the stops."

***

At the club, Johnny R met with Al Trent, who even at six in the morning looked well-groomed, and was dressed in his usual suit and tie.

"Mr. Richards doesn't think the problem lies in the quantity of the manpower, but the quality."

"What the hell does that mean? Joe Pullo ran the best crew in the city, but this Tanner, the bastard has more luck than I've ever seen. I mean he aced over a dozen guys last night, and he made off with a bundle of cash while he was at it. This shit is getting embarrassing!"

"Tanner is superb, we recognize that, and we're bringing in a man who's even better."

"Who?"

"Lars Gruber,"

"What? Wasn't that the name of the villain in *Die Hard?*"

Trent sighed.

"No, Lars Gruber is the best assassin in the world."

"Wait! You're talking about the German dude, right? Hell, he's better than Tanner, but he's in Europe."

"No, he's in California and should be finishing an assignment any day now, and when he does, he'll come here and kill Tanner."

Johnny snapped his fingers as he remembered something.

"Jackie Verona, the Underboss of the Calvino Family, Gruber killed Jackie's son when the kid turned snitch last year, didn't he?"

"Yes, and that man was guarded by US Marshals at a safe house. Tanner should be a walk in the park."

"Maybe so, but snitch or not, Jackie will want Gruber dead for what he did to his son."

"We're aware of that, Mr. Rossetti."

Johnny stared at Trent and understood.

"Jackie's days are numbered, aren't they? You're going to wrap him up in a bow for Gruber. What? Was that part of his compensation for coming here?"

"I never said that, but I will say this, if Mr. Verona changes his routine, or suddenly takes a vacation, I'll assure Mr. Richards that it was you who caused him to do so, and you'll be wearing your own bow, understood?"

"You're a real cocksucker, aren't you, Trent?"

Trent smiled without showing teeth, turned, and left the club.

CHAPTER 40 - Buddy, baffles, and bodyguards

Santa Barbara, California

John Mattson saw the classic Cadillac driving towards him and gave his partner, Harvey Cross, a nudge.

"Heads up," Mattson said.

He and Cross were bodyguards, and their current employer was a man who had refused to join The Conglomerate, although he didn't know it by that name, and later refused an offer to sell the same company.

The man had then been approached by a Conglomerate thug who was far less sophisticated than the business types he had seen before. The thug didn't touch him, but did give him a deadline to sell.

That deadline had come and gone, and since that day the man travelled nowhere without bodyguards, not even to the home of his mistress, which is where he had spent the night.

It was an upper-class neighborhood and the home was located in a cul-de-sac, where the houses had broad, sloping lawns, and wide driveways.

Harvey Cross had been dozing behind the wheel of the armored limo he drove while working, but looked up to see what had caught Mattson's attention.

"Hey, I know that car, that's Buddy's car."

"Who's Buddy?"

"He's a guy that hangs out at the sports bar I drink at, he said that old Caddy belonged to his father, it's a '61."

"He drives like he's drunk."

"He might be, he can really put it away."

The car in question was a convertible that had tail fins in the back. It was light purple with a white interior.

The car parked in a driveway across the street from the home Cross's employer slept in, and a blond man in his thirties staggered out and headed up the walk.

Cross lowered his window and called to him.

"Yo Buddy, you live here?"

Buddy turned and stared at Cross blankly, but then recognition dawned on his face, was accompanied by a wide smile, and Buddy walked over to the limo and peeked in.

"Harvey? What are you doing here?"

"I'm working. My employer is dating your neighbor."

Buddy laughed at that.

"Dating? You mean she's screwing him for favors. The wife and I always wondered how she afforded to rent that house."

Harvey waved a hand in an effort to disperse Buddy's breath.

"I see you closed down the bar."

"Yeah, and the wife is gonna give me shit."

Harvey pointed past Buddy to a woman standing in the doorway of the home where he had parked the vintage Caddy. The woman had her hair up in red curlers and wore a floral-print robe. She was looking at the car with a quizzical expression.

"Is that your wife?" Harvey said.

Buddy turned to look, then, swiveled back towards Harvey with a silenced gun in his hand, and when he spoke, his voice had a German accent.

"I've never seen that cow before in my life."

Buddy, who was actually Lars Gruber, shot Harvey and his partner Mattson a combined eight times, killing both men. The slaughter made surprisingly little noise, and the woman on the porch called to him, oblivious to what had just happened.

"Is this your car?"

It wasn't his car, but belonged to an eighty-year-old widower who was in the hospital. Gruber had taken the car from the man's garage and used it while he played the part of Buddy.

Gruber nodded to the woman while smiling, walked over, and shot her in the face. She fell backwards into her home, as a cat whizzed by her and ran off into the night.

Gruber looked around, that last shot made a bit of sound as the baffles within the silencer, which was a military grade sound suppressor, eroded from the heat of use, as he had employed it on his last three jobs.

While screwing a new silencer onto the gun, Gruber looked around to see if anyone was watching. No one was, and he marched across the street, where he carried out his assignment.

The victim's wife would be approached shortly after the funeral, and sell her late husband's company to a Conglomerate representative, but in the meantime, Gruber was headed to New York, his target, a man named Tanner.

CHAPTER 41 - Right back at ya

Rafe limped off the elevator and walked over to his car in the hotel's parking garage. Despite the fact that he was looking for him, he didn't spot Tanner until he was nearly at the car.

The garage was underground, and Rafe's car was near the ramp that led up to the street, where outside, the night was fading away to dawn.

"Are you making fun of my limp, or do you have one of your own now?"

"I underestimated a senior citizen, but let's talk in the car."

Rafe climbed behind the wheel while Tanner sat in the passenger seat. Tanner had dressed his wound and changed clothes. He was wearing jeans with a gray hoodie and running shoes.

"I watched the news before I left my room, it seems like the Giacconi Crime Family is in a war, the only thing is, no one seems to know for certain who they're fighting with, but for now, it's being blamed on the Russian mob."

"The reporters are behind the times, the Giacconi's and the Russians made peace years ago."

"A blog called *Street View* mentioned you by name yesterday, but the TV news anchors are saying that one man couldn't cause this much grief on the Giacconi's."

"They're right, because you helped me with Pullo's men."

"But all that chaos last night, that was you?"

"It was, and I'm not through yet."

"Johnny R?"

"Johnny R, or would you like the honor?"

Rafe smiled.

"My brother came out of his coma, so I've lost the fire in my belly, but I'll stay here for another day, and if you need help, just say the word."

"I was hoping you'd say that. I may need you for a diversion soon, likely tonight."

"I'm in, I still owe them for my brother."

Tanner opened his door to get out.

"Take care of that leg."

"Right back at ya," Rafe said, and Tanner limped up the ramp and was gone.

***

Tim and Madison stopped for breakfast after leaving MegaZenith, and Madison told Tim about her last conversation with Reese.

"When I told him I was quitting he asked for my phone number, can you believe that?"

"I don't blame him for trying."

Madison reached over and took Tim's hand.

"What are you doing today?"

"First, I'll get some sleep, but I'm meeting Tanner later,"

"Come back to my place. You can help me pack."

"Pack? Where are you going?"

Madison leaned across the table and gave Tim a long kiss.

"I go where you go, or haven't you noticed that I have a thing for you?"

"You'll really come with me? You know, where I'm going, it's far from the city. Hell, it's far from everything."

"I don't care. There's nothing holding me here anymore."

They finished their meal and made their way to Madison's apartment downtown, where they stood outside her doorway, kissing.

When they separated, Madison fished out her keys, and just as she opened the door, there came the sound of pounding footsteps.

Tim had just enough time to see that it was Carl Reese rushing towards him, before Reese collided with him and Madison, shoving them both inside and onto the floor.

Madison opened her mouth to scream, and Reese pointed a gun at her in warning, before slamming the door shut behind him with his foot.

Reese smiled at the couple.

"Now, it's time I heard the truth. Start talking."

CHAPTER 42 - What's good for the goose...

Tim helped Madison off the floor and then stood before her in an attempt to shield her from Carl Reese's gun.

Madison's apartment was modern, but small, and began with a living room, which was separated from a tiny kitchen by a waist high glass block wall. There was a sofa in front of the wall, and Reese gestured with the gun for Tim and Madison to sit on it.

Once they settled before him with their hands clasped together, Reese took a few steps to his right and gazed down the short hallway, where he glimpsed a view of Madison's bedroom.

He sent her a wink.

"You and I will explore that room later, but right now I want what you stole out of MegaZenith's computers."

Tim opened his mouth, but before he could speak, Reese raised a finger to his own lips.

"Don't give me any shit or lies, Timmy boy, just give me what I came for."

Tim released Madison's hand and reached into his side pocket. When his hand came out, it was holding a flash drive.

Reese ripped it from his hand and grinned.

"I don't know what's on here, but I would bet it'll make me rich."

"It's useless without the encryption key," Tim said.

"I doubt that, and I'd be willing to bet that MegaZenith's competitors will know how to crack the encryption."

"You got what you wanted, now just leave us alone," Madison said, and it broke Tim's heart to hear the fear in her voice.

Reese smiled a big happy grin as he sat in a loveseat across from the sofa, which was separated by a coffee table.

"Now that we got our business out of the way, let's say we have fun. Drew, what do you have to drink here?"

"What?"

"Refreshments, do you have any liquor?"

"No, just milk and soda,"

"Soda will do, be a good girl and pour three glasses for us, and if you come back in here with a knife in your hand I'll kneecap little Timmy, you get me?"

Madison nodded as tears glistened in her eyes. She went into the kitchen, poured cola into three glasses, and placed them on the glass block wall, which had a Formica counter atop it.

"Bring me my glass," Reese said.

Madison handed him one of the glasses and Reese smiled at her while his eyes roamed over her body.

"God, you are one hot little piece of ass, aren't you? Tell me Timmy, does she give good head? Oh never mind, I'll find out soon enough."

Madison backed away and Reese laughed again.

"Bring in those other drinks and sit them on the coffee table in front of me."

Madison went back into the kitchen and Reese drank his soda, as he swallowed the last of it, he leaned his head back, but his eyes never left Tim.

When the other two glasses were placed before him, he took out a baggie that held chunky white powder.

"I got a surprise, kiddies, something to spruce up your drinks."

"Cocaine?" Tim asked.

Madison shook her head.

"No, that's Rohypnol, ground up Rohypnol."

Tim stared at her in shock. Reese was about to do to them the very thing that they had once planned for him.

Reese laughed.

"Send that girl to the head of the class, yes sweet thing, these are roofies, and it's going to make you nice and friendly."

"I won't drink it," Madison said, as Reese divided the bag between the two glasses of soda.

Reese nodded.

"I thought you'd say that."

He stood, walked around the coffee table, and kicked Tim hard in the face, twice, splitting his bottom lip open.

Madison let out a shriek as Tim slid down the sofa, looking dazed.

"Drink bitch! Drink, or I'll keep kicking him until there's nothing left."

Madison picked up a glass, but had to calm herself before she could swallow.

"All of it," Reese said. "And you too, Timmy, it'll keep you nice and docile while Drew and I get to know each other."

Tim drank, but had to tilt his head sideways to keep it in his mouth, which seemed numbed and painful at the same time. He didn't taste the Rohypnol, but he did taste his own blood.

After they both drank, Reese sat back down and waited for the drug to take effect.

Madison grabbed a wad of tissues from a box on the coffee table and tended to Tim's busted lip, while standing in front of him. As she dabbed at the blood with one hand, she reached into her bra, and removed an empty foil packet.

She whispered to Tim.

"I drugged him too."

When Madison sat back beside him, Tim stared across at a grinning Carl Reese, and wondered who would pass out first.

CHAPTER 43 - Ewww, that's nasty

With Tanner rampaging throughout the city, Frank Richards decided to leave his Park Avenue apartment and retreat to his 35 acre estate located in the quaint hamlet of Katonah, New York, situated on the bank of the Cross River Reservoir.

He arrived there with ten highly trained bodyguards, and was confident that if Tanner made an appearance, the estate's security system would give them ample time to prepare. The home also had a panic room in the basement, and as a last resort, Richards could cower there until Tanner was killed or left the property.

Al Trent entered the massive living room and stopped short when he saw the painting hanging over the fireplace. It was much like the one Richards displayed at his Park Avenue apartment, but larger, giving it greater detail.

It was a portrait of Richards' late mother.

"Madison really does resemble your mother, sir,"

"That she does, but let's not speak of her. She's made her decision and she's no longer a part of my life."

"That saddens me. I had harbored a desire that she and I might one day wed."

"I knew you were attracted to her, but I didn't know you felt that strongly about her."

"She's a lovely girl, but it was more a desire to be a part of your family, since you've always been sort of a father to me."

Richards smirked.

"Careful Al, you're venturing into boot-licking territory."

Four guards remained outside to patrol the grounds, while the six remaining guards inside stood about. They were close, but not close enough to hear the conversation,

Richards settled himself behind an ornate desk with spindly legs and placed his briefcase atop it.

"I understand that Gruber finished his assignment in California. When can we expect him here?"

"His flight will be arriving soon, and he says that he already has an idea of how to kill Tanner."

"And what would that be?"

"He didn't go into detail, but I believe he'll be using Johnny Rossetti as bait."

"When you speak to him, assure him that Johnny would be an acceptable loss."

Trent smiled.

"I will do that with pleasure, sir."

"Has there been any sign of Tanner since he dispatched those men in the Bowery?"

"No sir, but we expect more trouble tonight."

"Lars Gruber will handle Tanner. Tanner's gifted at what he does, I'll give him that, but Gruber is far and away his better."

"He's certainly well compensated. I understand he asked for a quarter of a million dollars?"

"He did and I agreed to pay it. This nonsense has gone on long enough."

Trent gazed up at the portrait again.

"May I take a tour of the house, sir? I'll show myself around if you don't mind."

"That's fine, but don't be too long. Remember, you have to meet Gruber in the city. And while you're doing that, I'll be here working. Despite everything going on, I still have a corporation to run."

"Yes sir, I won't be long."

Trent went up the staircase. There were no servants in the home, as Richards had given them the next few days off. If Tanner did show, Richards didn't need witnesses around to view his capture and murder.

After opening three doors, Trent found the room he'd been looking for, Madison's bedroom. A room she mostly used during the summer.

Trent searched through a chest of drawers until he found her underwear. He removed a pink silk panty from the drawer, but then tossed it back in when his eyes found better treasure in the closet.

Behind a laundry basket was a pair of Madison's soiled panties. They were weeks old, and musky from use, but Trent inhaled them as if they were roses.

He stuffed them in his pocket, left the bedroom, and locked himself into an upstairs bathroom, where he used the panties while he pleasured himself.

It was as close as he'd ever get to being in Madison's pants.

CHAPTER 44 - One can only hope

LaGuardia Airport, Queens, New York

Lars Gruber tossed his carry-on bag to Johnny R's driver, Mario, and then cast a critical eye towards Merle and Earl, who were glancing about nervously.

"Who are these two losers?" Gruber asked in his normal voice, which had a distinct German accent.

"This is Merle and Earl Carter, Mr. Gruber. Johnny sent them along to keep an eye out for Tanner, these two know what he looks like."

Gruber laughed.

"Johnny Rossetti thought that Tanner would try to kill me? How would he even know I'm here?"

Mario shrugged.

"This dude Tanner always does what you'd least expect?"

"Nonsense, Tanner has no finesse. Frank Richards sent me a file on the man and it appears that he's just been lucky. Take that shootout last night as an example, the fool went up against seven men alone and walked away from it. Pure luck, but it's about to run out."

"You know best, Mr. Gruber," Mario said.

"I don't know best, fat man, I am the best. Richards is paying me a quarter of a million dollars to kill Tanner, and I won't even work up a sweat."

Merle's eyes boggled.

"A quarter mil? I thought the reward was only up to a hundred K?"

"That's for losers like you, I wouldn't get out of bed for that kind of money."

Gruber gazed at Merle and Earl again, and shook his head in disgust.

"Is this the best Johnny Rossetti has left? They look like frightened rabbits."

Earl frowned at that.

"Hell yeah, we're scared, Tanner ain't no joke."

Gruber made a sound of distaste.

"Schwuls!" Gruber snarled, using a German slang word to call the brothers homosexuals.

They left the arrivals area for private jets, and Gruber insisted on sitting alone in the rear of the limo, while saying that Merle and Earl weren't fit company. This caused Merle and Earl to sit up front with Mario, while Gruber sat in the back and opened the package that contained the weapons he would use.

As Mario put the vehicle in gear, Merle muttered, "Jerk,"

Mario whispered to him.

"Watch your mouth, Gruber is a dick, but he'll kill Tanner, count on it."

Earl smiled.

"My money is on Tanner."

"I'll take that bet for a hundred," Mario said, and Earl agreed.

Merle smiled.

"Either way we win, but maybe they'll kill each other."

"One can only hope," Mario whispered, as he drove back to Johnny R's club.

CHAPTER 45 - Psychosomatic

From the corner of his eye, Tim saw Madison act as if she were fighting sleep. At least he hoped it was an act.

As for himself, he felt no effect from the date-rape drug, but figured that would change. Taking Madison's cue, he blinked rapidly, lowered his head to his chest, and then jerked it up, as if to ward off drowsiness.

Carl Reese, seated across from them, was drugged as well, but it didn't seem to be affecting the man at all. He was a foot taller than Tim and weighed twice as much as Madison, and Tim realized that he would likely succumb last.

Reese spoke to Madison, who he knew as Drew.

"Why don't you take off your top, Drew, it'll save me the trouble."

"I'd rather play in traffic than have you touch me, pervert."

"Now, now, be nice. I could have had you two arrested for corporate espionage, but instead, I'm letting you keep your freedom. That's worth a row in the hay, hmm?"

Madison didn't answer, instead, she fluttered her eyes and her head lolled. It was no act, the Rohypnol in her system was kicking in.

Tim felt it as well, as his eyes seemed to want to close on their own, but a spike of adrenaline revived him temporarily.

He looked over at Reese and saw the man run a hand over his face as if to stifle a yawn, but then Reese rose to his feet, and walked around the coffee table to stand beside Madison.

"That's it sweet piece, get nice and drowsy, and you know what, you're gonna like it too. You've probably forgotten what it's like to be with a real man if Timmy here is what you're used to."

"He's twice the man you are," Madison said, but the words came out of her mouth like sap from a tree in winter.

She laid her head atop the sofa, but then jerked herself upright, as her eyes stayed half-closed.

Reese smiled down at her, but the smile became a yawn, and when he raised his hand to cover his mouth, he took a step backwards, as if stumbling. Afterwards, he went back to the loveseat and sat.

"Shit, you two are contagious, just watching you is making me sleepy."

Tim wanted to say something but found he couldn't muster more than a moan, as the drug came down on him like a hammer. He looked at Madison and saw that her head rested on her shoulder, and although her face was turned away from him, he could see that her mouth hung open.

Reese was holding the glass that had held his soda. He shook his head and blinked.

"Why am I getting drowsy? There's no way you could have switched glasses with me, and anyway, I drank mine first."

"Psychosomatic," Tim said, and was amazed at how much conscious effort it took to mutter that one word.

"Psychosomatic?" Reese repeated. "What, like it's all in my head?"

Tim nodded.

Reese stared back at him with a blank expression as he slid down lower in his seat.

A moment later, Reese sat up with a start.

"I'm really tired, but not too tired."

He rose, then, walked over and lifted Madison off the sofa by grabbing her around the waist. Madison made weak sounds of protest and moved her arms, but Reese pulled her along easily, dragging her towards the bedroom.

Tim stood, determined to stop Reese, only to fall to his knees, and then to the floor.

"Nooooo…," Tim said, but the sound barely carried, and Reese and Madison disappeared into the bedroom.

CHAPTER 46 - The envelope, please

Lars Gruber had Mario drop him ten blocks from the strip club and told him that he would enter through the back door when he arrived.

"When will that be?" Mario asked. "Johnny will be waiting."

"I'll arrive when I arrive, fat man, so just tell Johnny R to wait."

"Yes sir, Mr. Gruber," Mario said, and drove off with Merle and Earl.

The limo was barely out of sight when a red Mercedes pulled to the curb and Gruber climbed inside.

***

Not far away, Tanner was parked beside a fire hydrant, watching.

He had been following Johnny R's limo in the hope of catching the man unaware while on the road, and instead followed it to the airport.

He didn't know who Gruber was on sight, but knew that if Johnny R sent his limo to pick him up at the airport, then it meant he was a somebody.

After Gruber climbed into the second car, Tanner kept following, and in less than ten minutes, the car drove up a ramp and inside a warehouse that was once a box factory, but had several large FOR SALE signs across its front.

Tanner left his car in front of another hydrant and walked around to the rear of the building.

By the time he found a broken window that was close enough to hear what was being said, he had almost missed the action.

Jackie Verona, Underboss of the Calvino Crime Family was tied to a chair and gagged.

Verona was about fifty, in good shape, and had all his hair, which was still dark thanks to hair dye. In his youth, he had been a mob hit man, and was not above practicing his former trade when needed.

The man from the airport was standing before Verona and holding a gun, while three young punks looked on. No, make that two young punks, the third one was well dressed and the driver of the Mercedes, he wore glasses and had an air of authority about him.

He stood before Jackie Verona with the man from the airport as the other two watched and waited from several yards behind.

When the man with the gun spoke, Tanner heard the German accent.

"I want you to know that you were a gift to me. Your friends feared that you might interfere in my work here, and since your son was an informer, why not you?"

Jackie Verona mumbled and shook his head violently.

The German shrugged.

"Yes, but why take the chance, on your loyalty, or my life."

The man raised the gun and shot Verona once in the heart and once in the head, killing him. Afterwards, he removed the clip and handed the gun to the young man in glasses.

"I understand you have use for that weapon, Mr. Trent?" the German said.

"I do. It will be used to frame someone, insuring that this will never come back on you."

"And who would that someone be?"

"Johnny R, after all, it's due to his incompetence that we needed to hire you?"

Lars Gruber smiled.

"I see why Richards keeps you around."

"Thank you, and the best of luck with Tanner."

"It's not luck, I'm simply better than Tanner will ever be, I'm better than anyone."

Trent smiled.

"But not modest,"

"Never that," Gruber said, smiling.

Trent spoke to the punks as he handed them an envelope.

"You know what to do with the body, and once it's done, I suggest you leave town."

The punks nodded, looked inside the envelope, and smiled.

***

Tanner debated staying with Gruber, but decided to stick with the punks instead.

After Gruber and Trent left, Tanner watched the two punks move Jackie Verona's body from the chair and carry it to an old Pontiac that was sitting up on blocks behind the warehouse.

The car had no window glass left and its surface was more rust than paint. After opening the car's trunk, they dropped Verona's body in without ceremony and slammed the lid shut.

With that done, the punks walked over to a green Camaro with New Jersey plates and drove off.

Tanner walked back to his car, cruised around the area while thinking, and when he had a plan in mind, he drove back to the empty warehouse.

The lock on the back door gave him little resistance, and after going inside, he retrieved a white envelope from the floor. It was the white envelope that Al Trent had given the punks,

After backing his car up to the Pontiac, Tanner opened his trunk, and transferred Jackie Verona's body into it.

He knew the plan in his head was an elaborate one, but he also knew that if he could pull it off, that he would have The Conglomerate off his back, possibly for good.

Tanner drove along, laughing to himself, and looking forward to the night to come.

CHAPTER 47 - Kick a man when he's down

Gruber finally arrived at the club hours later, and let Johnny R in on his plan to kill Tanner.

They were in the office with Merle, Earl, and Mario.

"You're going to pretend to be me? How? I mean we're about the same size, but we don't have the same hair color and you look nothing like me."

"I don't have to be an exact match, I just have to give the impression that I'm you. I want you to leave the club, climb in the limo and go somewhere, somewhere big and busy, like a mall or a department store. I'll be there waiting for you, dressed exactly like you, and when I leave, I'll be flanked by four of your men, the bigger the better."

"And what do I do?"

"You stay where you are, or you leave by another exit, it won't matter, because if Tanner is watching, he'll think I'm you."

"What if he's not fooled?"

"Then, you will have to deal with that, but this is the plan. I spoke to Frank Richards on the drive in, and he approved it."

"I bet he did, he's probably hoping I'll get whacked first, but let's say your plan works, what happens then?"

"I come back here and wait for Tanner to make his move. He's a reckless fool and he'll be stupid enough to attempt to hit you here, despite all the men guarding you, possibly even because of it."

Johnny gave Gruber an incredulous look.

"I've got over a dozen guys here and dozens more coming. Do you really think Tanner is stupid enough to risk those odds?"

"It feeds Tanner's ego to defeat superior odds," Gruber said, before staring at Merle, Earl, and Mario, with disdain. "And from what I've seen of your men, he'll likely get past them, and when he does, he'll meet me and die."

Johnny looked Gruber over and smirked.

"What's so special about you, pal?"

"I'm the best killer in the world. That's what makes me special."

Johnny rubbed his chin as an idea occurred to him.

"How about a hospital, is that a busy enough place for you?"

"A hospital would be excellent. They'll likely have an awning outside and I'll be even harder to see as I make my way to the limo. And one more thing, we'll wear hats, that will cover my hair and obscure my face when I pretend to be you."

Mario asked a question.

"What hospital, Boss?"

"We're going to see Joe Pullo."

"That's good, it'll cheer him up."

Johnny nodded, but he wasn't thinking about cheer, he was thinking about revenge.

***

Tim awoke after being asleep for hours, and drifted in a haze of half-sleep as he tried to fight off the drug.

There was a puddle of drool under his chin and he dragged himself through it as he crawled towards the bedroom.

"Madison?"

There was no answer, and fear pushed Tim to his feet, to stumble along like a drunk. He was more tired than he could ever remember being, but it brought back a memory of when he was a child and his mother was still alive.

She had taken him to the city, his first time in New York, and they spent the day visiting The Bronx Zoo and the American Museum of Natural History. By the end of the day, he had a belly full of junk food and a mind filled with pleasant memories, but he was tired, he remembered that he was so tired, and that his mother had to carry him onto the train for their ride home.

That was a good tired, this was not, and he fought going under with everything he had. After what seemed like a millennium, he reached the bedroom doorway and saw that Madison was lying sideways across the bed. She was fully dressed, except for her blouse.

Reese was on his knees beside the bed with his arms outstretched atop the mattress, and in one hand, he clutched the blouse Madison had been wearing.

Reese was stirring as well, and he looked over at Tim with half-closed eyes and spoke.

"Drugged me... somehow... how?"

Tim ignored him, and after falling to his knees, he pulled himself up again by using the doorframe.

Reese rolled over until he was sitting on the floor with his back against the bed, and then fumbled at his waistband in an attempt to pull his gun free, but that simple task proved too much, and his hand dropped to the floor, as his eyes closed.

Tim tottered into the bathroom across the hall, where he collapsed onto the tile floor.

The feel of the cold, hard tiles against his cheek roused him, and he pulled himself up and over the lip of the bathtub. As he fell, the spigot cut his forehead, and the pain revived him further.

With fingers that felt numb, he turned on the faucet, and cold water rained down on him, causing him to shiver, but also granting wakefulness. He sat up inside the tub, shivering and breathing in and out quickly, then laughed as he realized he felt much better.

Fearing it wouldn't last, Tim scurried out of the tub, dripping wet, and looked for a weapon. When he returned to the bedroom, he was holding the lid off the back of the commode, and he stumbled over to Reese and brought the heavy porcelain crashing down atop the man's head, causing the lid to break in two.

Reese made a croaking sound and flopped sideways onto the floor.

Tim pulled the gun from Reese's belt, then, remembering the flash drive, he dug it out of Reese's side pocket.

With Reese handled, he sat on the bed beside Madison, who appeared to be asleep, the breasts beneath her red bra rising and falling in a steady even motion.

Tim realized he was drifting off again and went back to the shower. This time he was able to stand, and after only a few seconds under the cold stream, he went to the kitchen, leaving a trail of water in his wake, and prepared an insanely strong pot of coffee.

While he waited for the coffee to brew, he downed two energy drinks he'd found in the fridge, and took out his phone.

"Tanner."

"It's Tim, I need your help."

His words sounded slurred to his own ears, and Tim worked his mouth. Between the drug and the busted lip Reese had given him, he nearly mumbled.

"Tim? Where are you?"

Tim told him the street and described the apartment house, he hadn't noticed the street number when he arrived.

"We're on the second floor. It's Carl Reese, man, he followed us here and drugged us... but, but, Madison drugged him too."

"Where is Reese now?"

"He's here, unconscious, I smashed the toilet lid over his head."

"How much does he know?"

"He knows we're phonies, but not our real names."

"Was he armed?"

"Yeah, he had a gun. I took it from him."

"Tie him up, I'll be right there."

"What are you going to do with him?"

"I'm going to stick him in the trunk of an old Pontiac."

"What?"

"Nevermind,"

Tim took the time to sip some of the strong coffee before going back to the bedroom. Madison was mumbling and her eyes fluttered, as the effects of the drug waned.

Tim used scarves found in Madison's dresser drawer to tie Reese's hands together and lashed them to the headboard.

When he was finished, he glared down at Reese, and kicked the unconscious man hard in the balls.

Tim didn't know if Reese would feel it when he regained consciousness, but it made him feel better to do it.

CHAPTER 48 - Marone!

Tanner arrived in, of all things, a stolen flatbed truck with six portable toilets on the back. He parked it a block from the apartment and made his way there on foot.

He bent down and examined Reese, whose head sported a large lump.

"He'll be out for a while."

He then noticed the bandage on Tim's forehead, and the cut on his lip.

"He hit you?"

"The lip, yeah, but I cut my head falling into the tub."

Madison came out of the bathroom wearing a pink terrycloth robe and Tim handed her a second cup of coffee. Madison kissed him.

"My hero,"

"You're *my* hero, thank God you spiked his drink."

Tanner held his hand out.

"That text you sent me earlier said you downloaded Richards' files. Let me have the flash drive."

"Here, and I've got the whole thing in cloud storage too, but Tanner, I can't break the encryption."

"Try anyway, and you did good work, Tim, you and Madison both."

"We're heading to the place I told you about. I sent you the directions, but why don't you join us?"

"I can't. Not yet, I have to finish things here first."

"Are you talking about my father?" Madison asked, as she dried her hair with a towel.

Tanner shook his head.

"Not yet. Tonight I'm going to a club."

***

Inside Johnny R's strip club, Merle and Earl huddled in a bathroom stall together as they placed a call to Sara.

She was back home after being treated at the hospital for her head wound. The doctor had wanted her to stay for a day of observation, but she refused and decided to rest at home instead.

"Lars Gruber? Are you certain that's his name?"

"Yeah, why, you know him?" Merle asked.

"I know he's wanted by the FBI and Interpol for questioning in several murders. He's a hit man just like Tanner. I guess they've decided to fight fire with fire."

"Gruber's an asshole, but they say he's good, and Gruber thinks Tanner is coming to the club."

"Thank you guys, this news is worth a bonus, and be careful there. Just stay out of Tanner's way."

"That's our plan," Merle said.

When the call ended, Sara left her bed and got dressed, she too was going to a club.

***

At New York-Presbyterian Hospital, Johnny R visited with Joe Pullo.

Pullo sat up in bed with the right side of his chest bandaged, and an IV bag attached to his arm.

"How bad are you, buddy?"

"Shitty, but I'll heal, and I'm sorry, Johnny, but Tanner just outsmarted us."

"Don't be sorry. I know you, you did your best, but Tanner, he's inhuman."

"You should go away, Johnny, if you want to live, you should hide."

"Fuck that, but there's something I want to discuss."

"What's that?"

"First, how long are you going to be in here?"

"The docs want me to stay for a few days, but I'm bored out of my mind in here already."

"I hear you, but it sounds like you're lucky to be alive."

"Tanner could have easily killed me with the shotgun he had, but instead, he shot me with a pistol."

"Why?"

"We're friends,"

"Shit. With friends like him…"

"Yeah,"

"Listen up. Richards hired Lars Gruber to take out Tanner, but I'm not convinced he's up to it."

Pullo sighed.

"That's a toss up, Gruber's the best, at least he was. I think Tanner is going for that title."

"If Tanner kills Gruber, I'll be next in line, and I don't want to die."

"Richards will never cancel the contract on Tanner, and I don't think Richards would care if you were out of the picture too."

"I know that, Joe, and I've got a plan. Is there any way to contact Tanner?"

"He's made contact with me before, but I don't know how to reach him."

"Shit. I need to contact him, see if he'll deal."

"What do you have to offer?"

"I'll make sure he gets to Richards. That bastard is hunkered down in the country at his mansion."

"Tanner might take that deal, if I vouched for you, but you'd have to give your word not to touch him. At least for that one time,"

"I'd do it."

"Even though he killed your Uncle Al?"

"Yeah, because that hit was ordered by Richards. This whole mess lands at his feet."

"Let me think about it, maybe something will come to mind. I guess I know Tanner better than anyone, if that's even his real name."

Johnny slapped Joe on his good shoulder and headed towards the door.

"You know, Gino Maggio is one floor below you. He lost part of his right arm last night."

"Damn. Was it Tanner?"

"Yeah, but get this, Tanner tied off the wound with his belt. The docs say it saved Gino's life."

"I can see that. Tanner likes Gino."

Johnny R made a gesture towards heaven with his hands.

"Marone! If you and Gino are examples of what he does to people he likes, God help those he hates. See ya around, Joe."

Pullo said goodbye and then stared at the wall, while he thought about Tanner.

When he recalled something from years ago, he made a call.

"Hello?"

"Laurel Ivy, how are you, honey? This is Joe Pullo again."

CHAPTER 49 - O Romeo, Romeo

As the sun sank below the horizon, Lars Gruber gave instructions to the street soldiers gathered inside Johnny R's strip club.

They were all men that the arrogant German gazed upon with contempt.

What a motley looking crew.

Merle and Earl were towards the front. They were dressed in bulletproof vests, which they wore under hoodies, and were carrying guns in hip holsters. Of the eighty-two men present, they were two of only six given vests.

Gruber's trap relied on Tanner being able to enter the club, so that Gruber himself could kill him. To that end, he was going to lure Tanner in by understating their manpower. Merle and Earl would guard one end of the alleyway behind the club, while Mario, along with Carl the bartender, manned the other end.

Carl had been drafted because he knew Tanner on sight, but he was even less of a street soldier than Merle and Earl were, and looked to be on the verge of fainting as he sweated through his clothing.

Frank Richards was counting heavily on Johnny R being Tanner's next target, and so he gave the green light to Lars Gruber's plan.

For the next few nights, they would essentially control the city blocks surrounding the strip club, although to the uninitiated nothing would look any different.

Most of the men would be scattered away from the club in doorways and cars awaiting the sound of gunfire. Once they heard it, the entire area surrounding the club would be shut down, and no one would be allowed to leave until they were checked out.

To accomplish this, they had help from the cops, their cops, the ones they had owned for years. They had also stolen two work trucks from the gas company and dressed several men in coveralls and hardhats.

At the sound of gunfire, these trucks would block off the street leading to the club and tell anyone who asked that there was a gas leak.

They also had a van standing by, along with a freshly dug grave, and once Gruber killed Tanner, the corpse would be taken away within minutes.

Gruber's assessment of a motley crew wasn't far from the mark, because Tanner had single-handedly killed or wounded the best men Johnny R had, and so the word went out for replacements, and a variety of would-be tough guys showed up.

Several of the men in the club appeared to be street punks looking to make a reputation.

One in particular, was a guy in a leather vest who wore a black bolo tie with a silver clasp in the shape of an R. His spiky hair was dyed a white-blond and he had full-sleeve tattoos on both arms. He seemed to be dancing to music no one else could hear, and was annoying not only the other men, but also Gruber.

He popped his gum loudly and asked yet another question. He was no kid, but a man who had apparently never grown up.

"Those dudes with the vests, man, you're just using them as like... what do they call it, sacrificial sheep? I mean, you trying to get those dudes whacked or what?"

Gruber's face reddened as several men in the crowd mumbled their agreement with the punk's assessment, Merle and Earl among them, who were assigned to the east end of the alley. Other than a full-on frontal assault, the east end of the alley was the most likely place for Tanner to enter from.

Gruber raised his hands to indicate he wanted silence, and the gathering quieted down.

"The positions at the alley entrances and the front door are most vulnerable, yes, but that is why these men were supplied with vests."

The blond punk adjusted his mirrored sunglasses and let out a laugh.

"Them vests ain't gonna do shit for a head shot, yo!"

The crowd laughed, save for those wearing the vests, and Carl the bartender stumbled over to a stool, while feeling the need to sit before his knees gave out.

Gruber pointed at the mouthy punk.

"What's your name?"

"They call me Romeo, because I'm lucky with the ladies. By the way, where's all the bitches?"

"The strip club is closed, Mr. Romeo, but you are lucky."

"Why's that?"

Gruber smiled. It was a nice smile, and for more than a few, it had been their last sight on earth.

"We have one more vest left in the office. You'll be joining these two brothers here on the east end of the alley."

"Yo, that's bullshit, man!"

Gruber removed his silenced gun from the custom-made holster on his hip and held it loosely.

"Take it or leave it."

The punk sulked, but he stayed quiet.

"All right, now that we have settled that, everyone get into their positions, and remember, only these six—" Gruber smiled. "Only these seven men with vests stay near the club, the rest of you will be staying back, and when the shooting starts, you're to get into your designated positions and keep anyone from leaving the area. That way, if Tanner attempts to flee, he'll be trapped and I'll finish him off."

He gazed down at the men he had picked to guard the front door.

"If you hear trouble coming from the alleyway, ignore it and stay at your post. It could just be a diversion. I will handle the alley and the club alone. Now, everyone get going."

***

Sara parked her car five blocks from Johnny R's club and began walking there on foot. Her head still hurt from Tanner's assault, but the dizziness had abated, and if she walked slowly, she didn't weave.

Without knowing it, she passed by over a dozen men waiting to pounce on Tanner if he happened their way. And when she neared the strip club, she walked down a side street and huddled in the doorway of an abandoned factory, where she had difficulty finding a place to stand because of all the empty liquor bottles and trash in the shallow alcove.

The smell of urine was present as well, but Sara stayed, because from where she was standing, she could see the gate set in the fence, the fence at the east end of the alley that ran behind the club. A spot she also believed Tanner might pick as a point of entry.

Reaching into her purse, Sara removed her gun, and hoped for a chance at getting revenge.

***

On the other side of the gate, Merle and Earl found themselves standing in the well-lighted alley with Romeo, who insisted on showing the brothers his quick draw technique, as he drew and holstered his gun like a Wild West gunslinger.

"I ain't afraid of Tanner. Shit, let him come. I could use the reward money."

Merle spoke to Romeo as he looked about, his eyes searching up, down, left, and right for signs of trouble.

"Tanner is no joke, dude. We met him in Vegas and he almost killed us."

"Yeah, well, no offense, but you ain't me," Romeo said, as he danced to a tune only he heard.

Earl kicked a portable toilet that sat against the chain link fence. There was a thick padlock securing the door.

"They dropped this thing here and then forgot to take the damn lock off."

Romeo stopped dancing in place and ran back towards the club.

"I'll go see if Gruber has the key."

As Romeo neared the rear door of the club, he hollered to Gruber.

"Yo, Mr. G, we need the key for the portable shitter you had placed out here."

There was silence for several seconds, but then the door opened slowly. Along with new lighting, Gruber had Mario place convex mirrors on poles in the alley, so that he could see in either direction without exposing himself to a line of fire. To the west, the alley curved towards the avenue, while eastward, it stayed straight and dead-ended across from the rear of a warehouse.

The warehouse was made of red brick and had no windows at the rear. Inside, were two men hiding in the shadows, just in case Tanner sought to use the building's roof as a shooting post.

Gruber checked the mirrors, and when he saw Romeo standing alone, he peeked his head out.

"What are you talking about?"

Romeo pointed back the way he came, where Merle and Earl were.

"The portable shitter down there, it's locked. You got the key?"

Gruber squinted as he considered Romeo's words. He then disappeared back inside, only to return wearing his own vest and carrying a silenced pistol.

"Come with me, and for once, keep your mouth shut."

Romeo looked down at the gun in Gruber's hand and nodded.

Gruber moved down the alley at a steady pace, and as he neared their position, he waved Merle and Earl towards him.

"Come here men, we have to talk strategy."

The brothers approached warily, as they too stared at the gun in Gruber's hand.

When they were standing a foot in front of him, Gruber charged past them while firing shot after shot into the portable toilet. The *Clap, Clap, Clap, Clap, Clap, Clap* of his silenced shots making no more noise than a cough.

Gruber shot high and low, but seldom in the middle, and after emptying one clip, he reloaded in a blur of skilled motion and fired again.

After reloading once more, he approached the shredded plastic box at an angle, while walking sideways, his gun held at the ready. When he saw the lock on the door, he grabbed it with his bare hand and gave it a hard tug, causing it to come loose from the door. The lock had been cut and then glued back together.

Gruber ripped open the door and a bloody figure clad in black fell to the concrete of the alley. It had been a man, and he too had a vest, but it gave the man no protection against the numerous head and leg wounds acquired from Gruber's shots.

When Merle, Earl, and Romeo, gathered around Gruber, he holstered his weapon and gestured grandly at the corpse.

"Take a good look you worthless shits. There's your bogeyman Tanner, and now you know why I'm the best."

Romeo, who was actually Tanner in disguise, gazed down at the twice-killed corpse of Jackie Verona, and prepared to show Gruber the error of his ways.

CHAPTER 50 - Always the loner

Laurel Ivy took a seat by Joe Pullo's hospital bed after checking out his wound.

"That looks like good work. Who's your doctor?"

"You are, but the dude that sewed me up this time is named Patel. Don't ask me the first name, I can't pronounce it."

"I'm glad you called. I was wondering how you were."

"I called for a reason."

Laurel sighed.

"I figured as much, but if this is about Tanner again. I still have no idea where he is."

"And even if you did know you wouldn't tell me, right?"

"Yes," Laurel said, and then she gazed over her shoulder.

"It's just you and me, Laurel, so don't be nervous."

"Why would you think I'd know where Tanner is?"

"There was a period of time there when I thought something was going on between you two, am I wrong?"

"Tanner said something to you?"

Pullo laughed, but then winced at the pain of his wound.

"Oh, that's a good one, Tanner gossiping about his love life, no, he never said a thing, but like I said, I had a hunch."

"It's been over for a long time."

"I understand, but here's the thing, if, only if, you can somehow get a message to Tanner, do so. It could help him."

"I thought you were trying to kill him?"

"I was, but that's not what this is."

"What's the message?"

"Have him call me here."

"That's it?"

"That's it."

Laurel clasped her hands together in her lap, and she stared down at them as she thought things over.

"I wasn't lying when I said that I don't know where he is, but I might know someone that could reach him, and I'll ask that person to pass along your message, all right?"

Pullo smiled.

"That's great, baby,"

"If he calls…"

"Yeah?"

Laurel took in a deep breath and released it.

"Nevermind, if he wants to hear my voice or see me, he'll call."

"Being around Tanner isn't the safest place to be right now, you know?"

"He'll be all right, won't he?"

"I don't know, but if he calls me, maybe I can help."

"Even though he tried to kill you?"

"He didn't try to kill me, he just put me out of commission. Tanner never fails, and I think there's a German guy about to learn that the hard way."

***

Laurel left the hospital and took a cab to Rafe's hotel. When he opened the door and saw her standing there, shock lit his face.

"How did you know where to find me?"

"I'm nosey, and I'm careful. I went through the pockets of your pants while I was treating your leg wound and I saw the keycard for this room."

"Is there trouble?"

"No, but can I come in?"

Rafe let her into the room and she watched him walk.

"That limp seems better, how's the leg?"

"It is better, and I'm good thanks to you, but what's up?"

"I need to get in touch with Tanner."

"I don't know how to do that. He had asked me to help him tonight with this war he's raging, but he called earlier and said he wouldn't need me after all."

"But he might call again?"

"Possibly, but I have no way to reach him, and I'm headed home tomorrow,"

Laurel nibbled her bottom lip as she shook her head in frustration.

"Typical Tanner, always the loner," Laurel said.

Rafe smiled.

"You sound like you'd like to keep him company."

Laurel grinned back at him, but then she looked worried.

"I wonder why Tanner changed his plans."

Rafe shrugged.

"I guess he came up with a better one."

CHAPTER 51 - Tanner smiled

Tanner removed the bolo tie, even as his left foot came down on the back of Gruber's knee, driving him to the ground, he slipped the bolo over Gruber's head with one hand, while disarming him with the other.

Gruber reacted quickly as he tried to grab his gun, but only succeeded in knocking it to the ground. Meanwhile, the three fingers he managed to get between the bolo and his throat were being severed, and would soon fall to the ground.

The bolo was no mere tie, but a black garrote consisting of razor sharp wire at its middle, where it looped. Tanner forced a knee into Gruber's back, as he gripped the silver R and pulled tight on the bolo's ends, and the garrote pierced its leather covering, and sliced into Gruber's neck.

Merle and Earl looked on with wide unbelieving eyes as "Romeo" brought death to Gruber, but when Gruber reached back and swiped desperately at Romeo's face, dislodging the mirrored sunglasses, the brothers knew that they were looking into Tanner's eyes.

They gaped at each other in stark disbelief, before looking down at Jackie Verona's body in confusion, but then they gazed back up into Tanner's eyes, and knew it had all been a ruse.

Meanwhile, Gruber's panicked eyes pleaded with the brothers, as he pointed at them, silently begging them to help. The begging ended along with his life, as a powerful spray of blood erupted from Gruber's neck, and the German deflated like a defective blow-up doll.

Tanner's eyes never left the brothers, and he was ready to defend against them if needed, but Merle and Earl merely watched in fascination and horror. If they had any thoughts on trying to kill Tanner, they didn't act on them.

With Gruber dead, Tanner released his body and let it fall into the grime of the alley, while freeing the silver R from the garrote and pocketing it.

"Well boys, what do you say?"

Tanner stood relaxed, but looked like something from a Slasher movie, as Gruber's blood dripped off him, and covered half his neck and chest. He was armed, but his gun was holstered.

Merle and Earl looked at the guns on their own hips and shook their heads.

"We ain't killers, Tanner." Merle said. "It's why we didn't kill you back in Vegas, and we could have, ya know?"

"Give me your guns, slowly."

They did as commanded, and after chambering a round in each gun, Tanner removed and pocketed the clips, then, he handed them back with the empty clips that Gruber had used. After that, he picked up Gruber's gun and removed the silencer.

"What now?" Earl said.

"Now you boys get to be heroes, just shoot where I aim," Tanner said, and began firing into the soft dirt at the base of the wooden fence, which ran the length of the alley.

Merle and Earl followed Tanner's lead by firing off their chambered rounds and emptying their guns.

The clips Tanner had taken from Merle and Earl's guns were compatible, and Tanner removed the empty clip from Gruber's gun and fed in a fresh one before placing it near Gruber's body.

The sound of running feet came from the other end of the alley, and Tanner whispered to Merle and Earl.

"Let me do the talking."

He placed the mirrored sunglasses back on just as Mario and Carl appeared.

Mario spoke in a breathless gasp.

"Did we get him?"

Tanner was "Romeo" again, and as Romeo, he jumped up and down excitedly while pointing about.

"Oh shit man, shit man, shit man, he was hiding in the damn crapper, Tanner was hiding in there, and he, and he popped out and wrapped that wire around Gruber's neck. I didn't have a shot because Gruber was in front of me, but I tried to get him free and that's when all the blood sprayed. Tanner tossed Gruber at me and I kicked the door shut on him, and that's when these two lit his ass up inside the box."

Mario stared about at the carnage and then locked eyes on Merle and Earl.

"Wow, you guys killed Tanner?"

A noise came from behind them and they saw that Carl had fainted, he lay in the alley on his back. The sight of blood and death had been too much for him.

Mario checked him and saw that he was okay.

"He'll wake up soon, but stay here while I go get the dudes guarding the front door." Mario took three steps and then turned back. "Holy shit, Tanner and Gruber both, wow!"

Mario disappeared from sight and the gate in the fence creaked open. Tanner held his gun at his side, but at the ready, and saw Sara Blake peek in.

When Sara saw the bodies on the ground, she walked in, her mouth agape, her eyes locked on the bullet-riddled corpse clad in black.

"Tanner…?"

Tanner said, "Who's the bitch?" in his Romeo voice, which he pitched higher than his own, while also imbuing it with a singsong quality.

Merle and Earl moved towards Sara.

"You have to go now," Merle said, and he tried to push Sara back through the gate.

She broke free of him and bent closer to the bodies.

"Lars Gruber, Tanner killed him?"

"Yeah," Merle said. "But lady, Sara, you have to leave."

He looked over at Tanner and shook his head in a silent plea that he not kill her.

"This other body, the one with all the head wounds, is it really Tanner? Is he really dead?"

Tanner went into full Romeo mode and began prancing around.

"Hell yeah he's dead, my boys here blew his punk ass away after he killed Gruber."

Sara looked over at Romeo, who was turned sideways, and then she stared at Merle and Earl.

"You two killed Tanner?"

The boys said nothing, and Romeo filled the silence.

"They blasted his ass."

Sara huffed in surprise and took out her phone. Tanner thought she might call the police, the real police, and not The

Conglomerate's paid puppets, but instead, she was readying her camera.

Voices approached from down the alley and Merle and Earl grabbed her arms and dragged her outside the gate.

"You gotta go now, or they'll hurt you," Merle said in a desperate whisper.

Sara took one last look at what she believed was Tanner's body, and then she fled.

Mario returned with the guards from the front and Johnny R was with them. They came upon Carl first, and Johnny pointed at him.

"Oh no, Carl got killed too?"

Mario laughed.

"Nah, Carl just passed out from the sight of the blood."

Johnny smiled at that and continued on, where he bent down and examined the bodies.

"Fucking Tanner finally ran out of luck, and Gruber, whew, Tanner almost decapitated him."

He looked up at Romeo and saw all the blood covering him.

"Did you get wounded?"

"No man, that German dude went off like a fountain when I was trying to help him get free."

Johnny took out a phone.

"Bring in the van. We got two to go, but keep the street closed until I say different."

When he was done with the call, Johnny went over and stood before Merle and Earl.

"Boys, you just earned a fat reward, and I'll give you a night in the club you'll never forget."

Someone groaned, and everyone turned to see Carl sitting up.

Mario walked over and helped him to stand.

"Come on, tough guy, let's get you inside."

Johnny's phone rang and he answered it.

"Say that name again? A pause, "Yeah, bring her here. I'm in the alley."

He closed his phone and sighed.

"It looks like we may be planting three tonight. That so-called reporter is back, Sara Blake."

And while Merle and Earl blanched at the news of Sara's capture and coming demise, Tanner smiled.

CHAPTER 52 - It's been a hell of a night

The fence gate opened and Sara was shoved back into the alley by two thugs, one of whom passed her purse over to Johnny R.

"There's a piece in there, Boss,"

Johnny reached inside the bag.

"I'm more interested in her phone."

Tanner was leaning near the open gate in the fence, ready to move if necessary, and he wondered what Johnny would think if Sara had managed to take a picture earlier.

Johnny pushed several buttons on the phone, became frustrated, and tossed it over to Tanner.

"You look like you know how to search this thing, let me know if she's made any recent calls."

"You got it, Boss," Tanner said, and then he popped the gum he had in his mouth. He glanced at Sara over the tops of his shades, but saw that she was watching Johnny.

Tanner searched through her phone, and the results surprised him.

"There's nothing here. It's wiped clean, no call history, no photos, nuthin."

Johnny gave a little laugh.

"No, not nothing, she called someone and then erased it. Smart chick,"

The van pulled up outside, and Johnny told Mario and one of the men who came with Sara to tote the bodies into the van.

"But before you go..." Johnny said, and took out a knife, a switchblade. He knelt beside the body he believed to be Tanner's and cut open the left pant leg.

Tanner knew what he was looking for, and congratulated himself for having the foresight to prepare for it.

Jackie Verona's left leg had received several shots, but among the carnage they caused, Johnny could discern an earlier wound that laid beneath a bandage, a wound that was narrow and horizontal.

"Gino said he got the bastard with a knife in the thigh yesterday, and there's the mark. This was definitely Tanner. All right, take them away."

Mario pointed at Sara.

"What about her?"

"I'm sure her ride will be along soon. Who'd you call, honey, your Fed buddies?"

Sara tried to hide her surprise at Johnny's knowledge.

"Yes, I'm a former Fed, and Special Agent Jake Garner will be here any minute."

Johnny let out a sigh.

"Somebody turn on that hose by the wall and wash away this blood, and after that, soak everything down with bleach."

He grabbed Sara by the arm and guided her towards the club.

"Take off Mario, the Feds are coming."

Mario pointed at Tanner and the Carter brothers,

"You're with me guys, you too blood boy."

"Let me use the hose first," Tanner said.

After stripping down to the waist, he sprayed his neck and chest. He had to be careful about cleaning his arms, for fear that he might smear the temporary tattoos he wore.

A minute later, he was in the back of the van with a pair of body bags, a perforated Porta-potty, and two very scared brothers, as Mario drove them towards the tunnel.

Tanner grinned.

"It's been a hell of a night, hmm boys?"

Merle and Earl returned his smile with frowns.

CHAPTER 53 - Flirting with the enemy

Inside the strip club, Johnny R went behind the bar and poured himself a whiskey.

"What will you have honey?"

Sara looked surprised by the offer, but said she'd have the same, only on the rocks.

With the drinks made, Johnny leaned on the bar and smiled at her.

"You're a real looker, you got guts, and you're smart, a rare combination."

"Are you talking about me, or yourself?"

Johnny nearly spit out the sip of whiskey he had just taken.

"Ha, ex-Fed or not, I like you, and hey, that shit with Vince, that wasn't me."

"I settled with him."

This time Johnny nearly choked on his drink, and after coughing and wiping his mouth with the back of his hand, he pointed at her.

"That was you? You ordered that? There's a real dark side under all that beauty, isn't there?"

"Look who's talking,"

"Are you trying to flatter me honey?"

Sara said nothing, as she looked Johnny over and smiled. He returned her smile, and the silence between them stretched, as they admired each other.

The front door of the club banged open and Jake Garner walked in with two New York City police officers.

"Are you all right, Sara?"

"I'm good, but I'd like to leave."

"Where are the bodies?"

"They're gone. They were carted off in a white van that looks like a thousand others, and I never saw the plate numbers."

Johnny's face paled.

"Wait, what's he talking about?"

Sara smiled.

"You're thinking how could I have told him about the bodies when I didn't see them until after your men grabbed me, right? Well, it's very simple, I saw them earlier through a gap in that wooden fence."

Johnny finished his drink in one gulp.

"I don't know what you're talking about. I know nothing about any bodies, and I run a legitimate business here."

Garner laughed.

"I bet you've said those same words on many occasions."

Sara held out her hand.

"I'll take my purse now."

Johnny reached under the bar and came up with her purse. As he handed it to her, their hands touched, eliciting an inner sigh in each of them.

As Sara was leaving the club, Johnny called to her.

"Come back anytime honey, minus the Fed boyfriend of course,"

Sara smiled.

"Maybe I'll come see you on visiting days after your arrest."

Garner glared at Johnny, not liking the banter between him and Sara.

"She's leaving, but I'll be staying, and there's an FBI forensic crew on its way."

Johnny sent him a blank look.

"Whatever you say, Mr. Fed, but may I see the search warrants?"

"Those are on their way here as well."

Johnny had poured a second drink, and he held it up in a toast.

"Goodnight, Sara Blake,"

"Goodnight, Johnny R," Sara said, and out into the night she went, filled with a strange sense of loss, believing Tanner dead, and thus, leaving her devoid of her obsession.

CHAPTER 54 - Kiss or kill

Bass River, New Jersey 1:26 a.m.

Tanner watched Merle shovel the last pile of dirt atop the bodies, as Mario dragged over several branches to cover the grave.

Tanner was dressed in a T-shirt that advertised the strip club, and with his spiked blond hair, tight jeans, and tattoos, he looked younger than he was.

Soon, they were on the road headed back, but later, as they approached one of the rest stops on the Garden State Parkway, Mario pulled in and parked.

"I got to take a leak, anyone else?"

The others said no, and Mario climbed out of the van.

"I'll bring back coffee."

Mario went inside to use the bathroom, and while he was in there, Tanner spoke with Merle and Earl.

"You two are heroes now, but if you tell anybody that I'm still alive you'll be dead heroes, understand?"

Merle scowled at him.

"Hell, we ain't saying shit, Tanner, if they figured out we lied, they'd kill us."

"Tanner?" Earl said.

"What?"

"Are you gonna stay dead?"

"Who knows, I might grow to like it."

As he said he would, Mario returned with coffee, and they stood outside the van, stretching their legs while sipping their drinks.

Mario removed his wallet, counted out several bills, and passed them to Tanner.

"I called Johnny while I was inside and he said to pay you. As for Butch and Sundance here, Johnny's going to give them the hundred K reward tomorrow, along with one hell of a night at the club."

"We get the reward?" Merle said.

"Of course you do," Tanner said in his Romeo voice, but with an edge to it. "You killed Tanner, duh."

Mario looked at him and smiled.

"I haven't seen you around before Romeo, but you're all right. Come to the club sometime, I'm always there with Johnny, and we'll play some pool."

"I will, but next time have some women there too."

Mario laughed and slapped him on the shoulder.

"Come on guys, let's get back."

***

Tanner had Mario drop him off in midtown and then walked off towards Times Square.

Mario returned Tanner's wave goodbye and then pulled away from the curb.

Afterwards, he looked at Merle and Earl by using the rear view mirror.

"That dude is flaky, but he seems all right, hmm?"

"I hope I never see him again," Merle said.

"Amen to that," Earl said, "Amen to that,"

***

Tanner watched the van disappear and headed for the subway.

Tim had given him any info he had on Al Trent, and thirty minutes later, Tanner was breaking into Trent's Mercedes, where he left something hidden in the trunk.

When he walked away, he was headed back towards the subway, and limping noticeably.

He had given himself a cortisone shot before going to the club, but his hours of playing the dancing, prancing Romeo had made his leg hurt more than ever, and he knew he needed to rest it. He also needed time to think.

Tanner sighed as he settled into a seat on the subway.

There's plenty of time to think about things when you're dead, plenty of time.

***

In the office of *Street View*, Sara clicked on the icon marked POST and watched her blog entry go live, along with the single photo she'd been able to take in the alley, the one that appeared to show Tanner dead, while lying alongside Lars Gruber.

Behind her, Emily and Amy Sharpe let out a cheer.

"This is a huge exclusive, but we still haven't tied all this chaos back to MegaZenith," Emily said.

"I know," Sara said. "But I've become convinced that Frank Richards is involved. Too many things point to it."

Emily smiled.

"When do we get to meet those two brothers you told us about, the ones working undercover for you?"

"Maybe someday, but they can't be seen with us, not yet."

"Are they cute?" Emily said.

"Merle and Earl?"

The sisters nodded.

Sara grinned.

"I'll let you decide that when you meet them."

"They sound so brave, so smart," Amy said, and then she wondered why Sara was laughing.

***

The blog post spread across the Internet within hours, and by noon, the twenty-four hour news stations were discussing the photo, and debating if the mystery man named Tanner had really waged a one-man war on the mob, or was the dead man in the photo a scapegoat for a rival gang.

One thing was clear however, the blog and independent newspaper named *Street View* was once again worth reading.

***

Laurel Ivy opened the door of her illegal clinic and found Joe Pullo staring at her.

Pullo took one look at her red eyes and puffy face and knew he had guessed right about the depth of feelings she had for Tanner.

"I'm so sorry, honey, I know you had feelings for him."

Laurel opened his jacket and looked at his bandages.

"You should still be in the hospital."

"For what it's worth, Laurel, I think Tanner had feelings for you too. It's how I guessed that something was going on."

Laurel sobbed, as tears spilled down her cheeks.

"I loved him, Joe."

Pullo offered his good shoulder, and Laurel leaned in and cried on it.

***

At the club, Johnny R sat up on the sofa in his office as Al Trent walked in.

Trent handed Johnny the newspaper version of *Street View*, and jammed a finger at the picture.

"That is unacceptable. Are they going to arrest you?"

"Picture or not, there are no bodies, my lawyers say they can fight it."

"Why didn't you check her camera?"

"She didn't have one, she had a phone and it had no pictures on it."

"She likely sent them to herself or placed them in cloud storage."

"Phones can do that?"

"Of course,"

"I didn't know that. I'm old school."

"Mr. Richards is also extremely upset over the loss of Gruber. He was a valuable asset."

"He's blaming that on me?"

"Gruber was only involved in this because you were so ineffective at stopping Tanner. If you could run your own shop, Gruber would still be alive."

"Why are you here?"

Trent smiled, as his eyes twinkled behind his glasses.

"I'm here to give you a bit of news,"

"Which is?"

"You're being demoted."

"Say what?"

"It's simple. Mr. Richards will be recommending to the rest of the ruling council that you be relegated to an inferior position inside The Conglomerate."

"Only Sam Giacconi can remove me as Underboss."

"Sam Giacconi is a senile old man, and in any event, Mr. Richards seems confident that he can remove you as well."

"Bastard! Why doesn't he just have me killed like he did my uncle?"

Trent smiled again. "That was my recommendation, unfortunately, Mr. Richards ignored it."

Johnny was off the sofa and had Trent slammed up against the door before the younger man could even flinch. He took out his knife and pressed it against Trent's throat.

"I should slice you into pieces and toss you in the river."

Trent swallowed hard several times, but when he spoke, his voice sounded steady.

"If you hurt me, Richards *will* have you killed."

Johnny withdrew the knife, opened the door, and shoved Trent out into the hallway.

"Get the hell out of here!"

After slamming the door, Johnny picked up the newspaper and saw Sara's name and picture under the byline.

He laughed to himself as rival emotions surfaced.

He wanted to see Sara again, but when he did, he didn't know if he'd try to kiss her, or kill her.

"Maybe both," he muttered, and fell back onto the sofa.

***

Al Trent left the club in a huff, but as he drove away, his mood brightened.

He still had the gun that Gruber used to kill Jackie Verona, and it was time to play that card and have Johnny R framed for murder.

The gun was hidden inside his apartment, and after retrieving it, he planned to return to the club on some pretext and plant the weapon in Johnny's office.

However, Trent returned home to find a patrol car waiting for him, and the homicide detective accompanying the officers handed him a search warrant for both his car and residence.

"Are you serious? What is this about?"

"I'm investigating the murder of Carl Reese."

Trent thought the name sounded vaguely familiar, and then recalled it.

"Mr. Reese supervises the night cleaning staff for us. You're saying someone murdered him?"

The detective was a tall man in his fifties with graying hair, and he looked Trent over with suspicious and knowing eyes.

"An anonymous caller said that they saw you and Mr. Reese having an argument inside a warehouse yesterday."

"That's crazy, I barely know the—what warehouse?"

"It used to be a box factory. Mr. Reese was found shot to death inside the trunk of a nearby car."

Trent became silent as his mind raced through the possibilities. Someone was trying to frame him, but who? And what happened to Jackie Verona's body?

"I want a lawyer," Trent said.

The cop was not surprised by his request, and the murder weapon that Tanner had planted in his trunk hours earlier was discovered, and found to match the bullets that killed Carl Reese. It was the gun that Reese had used to threaten Tim and Madison.

Tanner had walked the still stunned Reese away from Madison's apartment the day before, as if escorting a drunk home. Afterward, Tanner had driven Reese to the former box factory, where he shoved him inside the trunk of the Pontiac and shot him with his own gun.

Reese had pleaded with Tanner for his life, but it fell on deaf ears.

As if the attempted rape of Madison wasn't reason enough to kill him, Reese also knew that The Conglomerate's computers had been compromised by Tim, and so had to die.

In the coming days, a forensic team would discover one of Al Trent's hairs in the warehouse, a single strand left behind when he was there with Gruber.

While an envelope found with Reese's body would be confirmed as having Trent's prints on it.

A second gun found in Trent's apartment won't be linked to any crimes, but two shell casings recovered inside the warehouse will match the gun perfectly, and cause the police to wonder if it had been used to create the dried puddle of blood found beneath an equally bloody chair.

When Johnny R learned of Trent's troubles, he wore a smile for days.

***

On East 6th Street, Mrs. Edith Ross opened her apartment door and smiled at her young neighbor, Ms. Claire Harper.

"Hello dear, how are things?"

Claire looked disheartened.

"Things are awful. My renters insurance won't cover all the damages, the police are still calling my apartment a crime scene, and the landlord says that he doesn't know when I'll be able to move back in."

Mrs. Ross looked sympathetic. The old woman also felt a sense of guilt over having let the young man with the family photo fool her. Had she called the police or the landlord to confirm his identity, Claire could have avoided all the trouble she's been going through since returning from her vacation.

The old widow invited Claire inside and they talked over coffee. But as Claire was leaving, she remembered the main reason that she had dropped by.

"You said that a package came for me?" Claire asked.

"Oh yes, this came yesterday,"

Mrs. Ross reached over to a table by the door and handed Claire a package that was about twice the size of a cigar box. It was wrapped in plain brown paper, postmarked New York City, and had a fictitious return address.

"I don't know what this could be, but thank you for holding it for me."

"You're welcome, dear, and how are your parents?"

"They're great, but it's a little weird being back in my old bedroom."

"The next time I speak to the landlord I'll try to light a fire under him. I miss having you in the building."

Claire kissed the old woman goodbye on the cheek, and returned to her car. She was just about to start the engine when curiosity took hold, and she decided to open the package instead.

Inside, was a rectangular metal box, and taped atop the box was a note:

Sorry for the mess, I hope this makes up for it.

When Claire opened the box, she saw that it contained thirty-thousand dollars in cash.

It was a large chunk of the money Tanner had stolen from The Conglomerate drug den he had attacked days earlier.

Despite the horror show she returned home to after her apartment had become a battleground for Tanner and Joe Pullo's crew, Claire had enjoyed a very lovely time while on her Mexican vacation.

Next year, she was going to Hawaii.

CHAPTER 55 - I wouldn't miss it for the world

The farm was as isolated and large as Tim had promised it would be, enabling Tanner to hone his long distance target shooting skills.

The limp in his leg had gone, and he wiped off the temporary tattoos with rubbing alcohol, but some of the hair dye remained, particularly along the sides, and Madison quipped that it made him look distinguished.

The old farmhouse was huge with six large bedrooms, and Tanner took the one farthest from Tim and Madison, giving them their privacy, and insuring his own.

The Conglomerate thought he was dead and had no idea that he possessed their organization's files. Tim was undoubtedly still being sought, but he would no longer be using the handle Rom Warrior and was working exclusively on cracking The Conglomerate's encryption.

As for Madison, her only family, her father, had disowned her, and had no reason to track her down.

***

Days after coming to the farm, Tanner was lying prone on his stomach atop a grassy hill, sighting a long-distance shot, when Tim approached from behind.

Tim gestured at the shooting earmuffs Tanner removed as he stood to greet him.

"How did you hear me coming with those on?"

Tanner pointed at the thermos of coffee he'd brought with him to practice shooting. It was shiny, and better yet, reflective.

Tim smiled.

"That's why you told Madison to make sure she bought the type made of stainless steel, you could see my reflection. You don't miss a trick, do you?"

"If I did, I'd really be dead. What's up?"

"The daily progress report, I'm still unable to break their encryption, but as I said before, it would be the greatest of luck if we stumbled onto the correct sequence randomly."

"I get that, I also think you wouldn't climb up the hill just to tell me that again."

Tim took a folded piece of paper out of his shirt pocket.

Tanner opened the paper and saw a list of names. He recognized a few from the news, and Frank Richards was also on the list. The heading at the top gave a time in the near future, and the place was a building on Wall Street in New York City.

"What's this?"

"You can thank Madison for that. She bagged up the debris from the office shredder and spent the last few days piecing that and two other sheets together. The other sheets turned out to be nothing, but that, that's a list of The Conglomerate ruling council and the time and place that they'll be gathering."

Tanner looked thoughtful for a few moments, but then nodded to himself, as an idea came to mind.

"The next time we go into town, I'll be shopping for a business suit."

Tim looked puzzled for a moment, and then appeared stunned.

"You're planning on going to that meeting?"

Tanner was still holding his rifle, and he stroked it like a lover.

"I wouldn't miss it for the world."

A PLEA

Thank you, precious reader, for spending time with Tanner. I hope you enjoyed the book. If you did, please consider writing a review. Without reviews, an author's books are virtually invisible on the retail sites. Let other readers know what you thought! You can leave a review by visiting the book's page, and I will greatly appreciate it.

—Remington Kane

LEARN ABOUT NEW RELEASES FROM
REMINGTON KANE

http://www.remingtonkane.com/contact.html

MAKING A KILLING ON WALL STREET - A TANNER NOVEL

COMING IN MARCH 2015

TO CONTACT:

www.remingtonkane.com

tannerseries@gmail.com